Amy The Elf And Her Friends

by

Stephen Paget

Copyright © 2023 Stephen Paget

ISBN: 978-1-916981-28-7

All rights reserved, including the right to reproduce this book, or portions thereof in any form. No part of this text may be reproduced, transmitted, downloaded, decompiled, reverse engineered, or stored, in any form or introduced into any information storage and retrieval system, in any form or by any means, whether electronic or mechanical without the express written permission of the author.

INTRODUCTION

Howdy there, I'm the author Stephen Paget.

Before reading, I have a confession to make. I'm not the world's best storyteller.

My dream goal ever since I was a child was to be a cartoonist and a book author. But I suffered too hard from writer's block. I grew up with an older brother and two sisters. (One younger, one older.) They can tell you the unfunny comics I used to come up with.

As I became an adult, I read over 400 webcomics (yes really), actually read books (again, yes really), and battled with my short attention span watching movies, (I'm disabled and been diagnosed with two speaking disabilities. Asperger Syndrome and Semantic Pragmatic Disorder. Having Asperger Syndrome means having a short attention span.) all to look for inspiration.

The following stories were written from 2021 to 2023. And come from me trying to put these characters of mine into laughable situations for at least 19 years. Part of me just wanted to give up and say I just didn't have the talent.

But no…..I like to think I had some talent writing stories. Before writing this, I was a fanfiction writer and for many of the 125 stories I wrote, although the reviews I got were few. Many praised me and told me I was a hilarious storyteller. Even my bad and flawed stories got positive reviews.

If I was doomed to die, I wanted to die accomplishing my goal, whether it was good or bad. I went back and forth with my characters many, many times with my characters trying to make a story that's at least presentable.

Even bad stories can be entertaining. And when I wrote these stories. I did have the idea of making them somewhat hilariously stupid. I decided to take the Trey Parker and

Matt Stone approach of writing stories which I once read in a South Park book.

"Don't think of your plot for very long. Just think stupid and have fun."

And that's what I did. Depending on your sense of humour. What I did will either be good, be hilariously stupid bad or just plain bad.

And if people thought it was plain bad. I figured so be it. Everybody has different tastes. I've seen hilariously bad fanfic authors become well famous and liked because of bad scathing reviews on the internet.

What you are about to read combines what I originally intended as four books. I intended to call them "The World Of Clastonia and the Magic Books", "Amy the elf sorceress and her friends.", "The ex-bully who wanted to be loved." and "Dougal's non-contagious werewolf girlfriend." I have combined them all into one book for you to read. I figured loads of people don't read books anyway and just decided I'd give them every idea, and for dirt cheap! Lucky you.

I gave the title of this book the title of my second originally intended book to give the main character more recognition and for more people to recognize as a parody.

The main character is meant to have a generic, somewhat naff name to make her look like an extremely unlikely hero.

What I did will either offend you, or it might make you laugh more than any well written comedy.

Good luck and look both ways before crossing the street.

Stephen Paget.

For all my family and friends.

Special thanks to all the inspirations that made this story possible!

Family Guy (Its humour is an inspiration. The early seasons that is. I now think the show is godawful.)

South Park (Its humour is also an inspiration.)

Red Dwarf (Its humour is an inspiration. I thank both the T.V show and the books which are different from the show.)

The Simon the Sorcerer adventure computer games. (Simon himself is a human transported to another dimension. I even thank the 3d, 4 and 5 games which everybody hates.)

Super Mario Bros. video games (Bowser is partially an inspiration for Phobix and his kids inspired Snork and Snerk. Amy's personality is brave like Mario's and Misty is shy like Luigi.)

Street Fighter (M . Bison is also an inspiration for Phobix. Some of Ryu's personality may have become Amy's.)

What was the name of that book with the woman who could turn into a tree creature? And decided that life wasn't right for her. I think the author's first name was Celica… damn it this is gonna really kill me……

The book Memo the Hierophant. (Thorak's name is based on a robot character named Thorax.)

The Lily Quench Book series (Lily's looks and personality are an inspiration for Amy.)

The cartoons Blazing Dragons by Nelvana and Dragon Tales by PBS. (Inspirations for Thorak and Rufus.)

The Book Muddle Earth by Paul Stewart and Chris Riddell. (Its parody and fantasy is an inspiration. And its design of goblins inspired Norman and Garrett. I've actually read the book and not seen the CBBC series.)

The over 400 different webcomics I've read when I was unemployed. That's not a joke and an exaggeration. I really have done that. Isn't it a bummer that only a third of autistic people have jobs? Wow….I'm a low statistic. Wanna know what the worst webcomic ever made is? Don't ever read Kit and Kay Boodle. Also, I think Sabrina from Sabrina online and her raccoon boyfriend was an inspiration for Amy and Dougal's personality.

The movie Downfall and its many parodies.

Jenny Nimmo's book "The dragon's child." Inspiration for Dougal and Thorak's friendship.

Myself (Dougal is based on me. But loosely. We both have Asperger's Syndrome.)

The Spyro the dragon games – Made my love for fantasy even higher. I've also read a lot of fanfiction about Spyro that inspired my stories. Looking at you Panthergirl!

That's about all I can remember………..I thank anybody and anything I missed.

BOOK 1

The World of Clastonia and the Magic Books.

Chapter 1

Once upon a time……far, far, away in an alternative dimension. There lived a universe and a world that went by the name of Clastonia. It was a strange universe that had both anthropomorphic and non anthropomorphic animals along with fantasy creatures such as elves, goblins and dragons and where humans were about as rare as pandas on Earth.

It was a world where the people were much more advanced than humans on Earth and had invented guns a few generations ahead of time, skipping wars with knights in armour and swords.

It was also a world where magic had a mysterious, but somewhat explainable origin.

Greetings viewer……..before we start. There are five main characters in this story.

Amy Woolruffe : A tall, cute orange skinned, blonde haired, young adult elf. She works as a librarian in the city of Sunchester across from the village of Ferlock where she resides. She is gold hearted, but believes in being strong and not a pushover. Her age is 26.

Misty Woolruffe : Amy's younger sister. Although she and Amy are twins. Misty dyed her hair a brunette colour when she was six and put her hair in a different style so that she and Amy could be told apart. She can be immature and unladylike at times, but does have a good heart like her sister. Being Amy's twin sister her age is of course 26.

Dougal John McKenzall O'Ryan : A young human adult who once lived on Earth. Was teleported from Earth to Clastonia as a baby through magic in a machine that was designed to see if there was life on other planets. When the machine only produced a baby human. The baby was adopted by an anthropomorphic sheep who went by the name of Ralph. As well as his talking sheep father, Dougal also lives with a friendly dragon called Thorak. Being in a world where humans are a rare species, this has made him shy and somewhat insecure. We will read more on his origins later. He once lived in Scotland. (Based on the fact the author is Scottish.) His age is 25.

Thorak O'Ryan : A tall slim green dragon with spiky green hair very similar to the colour of his skin. Like the fierce dragons you read in stories, he is a tall height but only silently more taller than a human. He wears a red T-shirt with a smiling yellow face on it. He is Dougal's adopted brother/pet/best friend. In Clastonia, dragons are somewhat accepted amongst Clastonia's wide variety of species. He was found as an egg by Ralph who was doing bird watching and thought he was a bird. When he hatched to be a dragon. Ralph still adopted him. Reading once that dragons developed fire breath magically when they turn 18 and sharp teeth much later in life helped his decision. Being raised by Ralph's kindness has made Thorak gentle. He is one of the few friends of Dougal, as Dougal is somewhat shy and ridiculed for being a rare species. Thorak is feared for being a dragon, making the two very good friends.

Although Thorak has no wings, he can still fly. His age is 24.

His name is based on Thorax, a metal robot gangster shaped like an insect in a series of comics, Ralph read as a child.

Whether one can call Thorak a brother or pet of Dougal is somewhat debated. As well as them being different species, Thorak is keen to go on walks like a dog, has played frisbee with Dougal before and when dared once ate dog food to see how his immune system was1 to food.

Sadly to say the toilet got clogged and Dougal had to clear the toilet wearing a gas mask.

And finally the last one……

Garrett Brettson : An orange skinned, blond haired, small grumpy muscular blonde haired pessimistic goblin who Misty dates also. Although grumpy he does have a good heart. He has an uncle called Norman. Has a tail with a brown tuft of hair at the end similar to a lion's.

Not a main character but worth mentioning….

Norman Brettson :Like Garrett, he is a small grumpy pessimistic goblin. Wears a blue magic hat that can contain any item no matter how big. Is bald. His age is 46. Not evil but does have some bad manners and bad taste. Wears a blue shirt and brown trousers.

Let's begin…….

"Hey! Hey! Stop!" Norman snarled.

Eh?

"Is that all you have to say about me, author? You gave me just a few sentences!" Norman snarled.

Very well, how about your hygiene is terrible and you're a slob?

Norman thought it over. "I'll be good." He groaned.

Anyhow……let's begin.

In fantasy stories, one might read about powerful wizards (or sorceresses we're not sexist in this story) and magicians wielding huge books of magic. Feared amongst many for their knowledge of magic. But here's what's never explained in these stories. What are the origins of magic? And how was it ever learned and taught in the first place?

The present day of Clastonia takes place in 1622. You might think that's a sucky year, but you forget that this is Clastonia not Earth. People in Clastonia were much more advanced than humans on Earth. Unlike Earth, inventions for the peace and quiet we have on Earth today were invented way more earlier. As well as a fact that's it's not considered a miracle to live beyond the age of 30. Television and video games do exist in Clastonia, so for all lazy slobs, you can chill out. Looking at you, Norman!

"Hey!"

Even though most of the further stories said later will take place in 1622. Let's go back 820 years to the year of 802. Oh by the way, the world of Clastonia has actually been around more than 1622 years. They ACTUALLY

HAVE RELIGION! Their version of Jesus is very similar to ours. You wanna hear the differences? For starters…….

"Get on with the story!" Norman yelled.

Alright…..keep your pants on.

"Not wearing any." Norman grinned.

Ewww……..well ANYWAY. 820 years ago. When it was discovered hip to wear your underpants above your trousers and kids did it. (Including females.) Random books of magic were discovered lying out in the middle of random places, as if…   by magic. They weren't very many of them. Around twenty were discovered and the width of the books varied. One only had 6 pages, some had twenty and one was reported to be as high as 60! Through out the books although some of the spells remained the same, most differed.

What were the spells of these books. Well throughout these twenty books, many of the spells discovered had mainly useless spells and they were different for everyone. One spell could make random flowers appear in your hand. One spell could give you a ten gold coins off voucher off a can of spam in Wesco. For spam lovers you might think that's not so bad but according to the words in the book, the spell could only be summoned once every three months. Or how about a spell where you could summon random rocks? Or summon tiny shampoo bottles only slightly smaller than a mouse?

And for this time period let's introduce Rubert. He is a goblin who is Norman the goblin's ancestor. And is a citizen of the village of Ferlock. He himself was not happy with the useless spells and proceeded to burn the book, but to his surprise the book was indestructible. And so was the tiny magic scepter that came with it. The spells could only be activated by the scepter not with hands.

It turns out later on however he was glad he didn't burn the book! It was discovered that new random spells got added magically to the books. The time periods varied sometimes it was a day, sometimes it was a month and sometimes it was fifty years. (More on that later.)

One of the other people who had discovered the books was an elf who also lived in the village of Ferlock, his name was Colin Woolruffe and he was the ancestor of the elves Amy and Misty. Colin however had a more useful set of spells. One of the spells allowed him to duplicate any object he wanted. Even money. And even a book of magic, and indeed he did do this. But when this happened for whatever reason it wasn't the same as the book he had discovered while walking in the woods one day. The book only had three pages. And the spells were all useless. If you want a clue how useless they are. One spell was for summoning the ear wax only found in a goblin's ear and summoning a pair of underpants that were similar to how they looked like if an ogre had been wearing them for three days straight.

After receiving permission from the mayor, he was going to sell the book in his general store. But Colin had somewhat of a conscience. What would magic do in the wrong hands? So he decided to sell the duplicate book for a million gold coins. Something that nobody would pay money for.

Colin didn't do this because he was greedy. Gold coins could be found everywhere. Mostly in metal boxes hovering above the sky. Throughout Clastonia, there were random metal boxes levitated in the sky, and when they had a G on it, when punched by one's fist hard it produced a gold coin and then disappeared. (If it didn't have a G on it, it just disappeared.) These boxes appeared anywhere day after day and were even longer than the magic books.

It sounds a little similar to how a game on Earth called Super Mario Bros. does these coin boxes doesn't it? (Please don't sue, Nintendo.)

Anyway......over 800 years passed and the magic books evolved, and boy did they evolve......the most infamous being the dark, destructive magic of the queen of monsters. Queen Phobix Blackspark of the monster city of Deathstar in the country of Monstropolis a short distance from Wales. (Deathstar is not the actual city's name, but changed to make citizens fear their ruler.)

END OF CHAPTER 1

Chapter 2

Phobix was a monster, and not just monster as in personality, a LITERAL monster in appearance, she had a human like body with yellow skin and a head shaped like a star. She wore a long red dress that needed to be zipped from the back. One would think that they would be honored to zip the dress up in her back. But if one saw her wrinkly back from her 70 years of age. They might throw up. Not that Phobix needed someone to zip her dress as she could do it with her magic.

She had two monster servants who took care of her every command. They were brothers and their names were Snork and Snerk Von Snaffler.

Snork was a monster who had a blue skinned human like body and had dark blue spots on his stomach. He had a big nose, horns, no hair and one of his eyes stuck out in long sockets out of his head. He had a tail that stuck out of a pair of dark denim shorts he wore. At the end of the tail was a tuft of hair similar to a lion's.

Snerk, his brother, was shorter than his brother, he looked like a red circle missing its bottom with fat muscular arms. Like Snork, he had horns on at the top of his head. One eye sticking out in long sockets, and dark spots around his stomach area (only they were dark red and not dark blue like Snork's) at the bottom of his body he had tentacles like a octopus. Unlike Snork he had no tail.

The brothers served the queen well, and were the only two Queen Phobix respected.

Over 800 years ago, one of the books of magic was discovered by Phobix's ancestors. This was the book with 60 pages of magic. And over the years it had evolved, the magic had evolved into destructive dark magic, Phobix could shoot lightning from her sceptre with just a few words, she could levitate and control heavy objects with only a few words and she could even control her age and bring the dead back to life. She had spells who could make an evil clone out of anybody. (Though she was yet to try this.) She was feared and respected by every monster in the city she controlled.

She was responsible for many dark acts, murdering monsters and mutilating them in bloody destructive ways who didn't agree with her. She was just like her ancestors who in the past had many battles with monsters and non-monsters. Good had always triumphed over evil, with the other books of magic with her ancestors and thanks to robots being designed by Alec the goblin three hundred years ago. (Another Norman the goblin ancestor.) Robots with four chainguns, and all sorts of deadly weapons had been invented. More than a hundred years ago, as robots got more commonplace. The military got abandoned by citizens in a lot of countries and almost completed replaced by robots. (But not all.) Designed to eliminate any threat. Whether monster or non-monster. Phobix still used her people and dark magic as she believed it to be more powerful than any robot.

Peace had reigned for over a hundred years but that was about to change, Phobix discovered a new spell in her book that would allow her to rain huge meteors on a city. She tried it out in a city called Sunchester. And watched in laughter as the city turned into rumble. She would rule the world!

Or would she?

Amy the elf was travelling by car to her job as a librarian, although she could teleport by magic, she used a car as she didn't want to frighten anybody by using her teleport spell. She watched in shock just outside Sunchester as the city fell into ruin from the meteors. She had her mouth wide open in shock. She had her book of magic with her.

She suddenly thought of an idea.

She parked the car on the side of the road got outside, and pointed her scepter to the ruined city. She opened her book and found the undo spell. She flipped her scepter on by a switch. (Yes, in this story, scepters have on and off switches and don't require batteries.)

"Undo this damage!" she yelled.

Suddenly in reverse meteors flew out the city, and the city came back to life. Amy had undid all the damage from the meteors. And became an unlikely heroine.

As for Phobix, she watched in shock and saw all her damage get undone.

That night she went to a bar and got drunk. When the news came out that an elf had saved the city with the magic book from her ancestors. She was not a happy monster.

"I want that BOOK!" she snarled.

Chapter 3

The origins of Dougal McKenzall O'Ryan.

The following story takes place in 1597, twenty five years before the present day of Clastonia, Norman and his brother Alex are in their 20's in this story.

Alex the goblin (not to be confused with his ancestor Alec) visited his brother Norman and asked him to look after his house.

Unlike Norman, Alex was much more polite and tidy than his younger brother and smarter too. He did work for WASA, which was Clastonia's version of NASA.

Before we go into Norman looking after Alex's house. Let's explore WASA a little bit.

In WASA a huge machine had been invented to detect any life outside the world of Clastonia. WASA as well as inventing a large machine, that would detect any alien outside of Clastonia. They had invented a satellite that floated around in space that would detect any life on another planet.

The machine had been invented 53 years ago in 1569. When the alien detector machine had been turned on the first day in July 22th. (Yes in Clastonia, months still have the same names.) the machine had succeeded in detected life on planets. A mixture of panic, shock and excitement had hit WASA, but then the machine reported that the life seen was life on Clastonia, which then made everybody extremely annoyed.

The machine had broke down, and Alex a talented mechanic had been called to deal with the machine. The work was long and extremely hard. The machine was huge and many parts had to be repaired. It was after hours and Alex still hadn't fully repaired it.

A green three eyed ogre with brown hair and dressed smartly in a tie, shirt and black trousers came over to Alex. He was his boss.

"Hey, it's after 5pm." The boss said to Alex.

"What, oh man! I've been doing so much, and I'm on holiday next week! Hey, do you want to cancel vacation time, to work on it?" Alex asked.

"Alex, an ogre with big sharp teeth I may be……."

"All the better to eat me with!" Alex interrupted joking.

The boss ogre continued frowning. "But I'm not sadistic. You still need to take your vacation. We don't desperately need this machine. It hasn't detected anything in over 50 years."

"Do you think I could take it home and work with it over my holiday?"

The boss thought this absurd. "Take it home? How? It's a huge heavy machine!" he shouted.

"By my brother's book of magic, it can teleport and even levitate heavy objects! I borrowed this off him."

"Don't bring books of magic into work! They're dangerous!" the boss yelled angrily.

Alex shook at the boss' anger and loud voice. "Sorry." He shook.

"It's alright. Just don't do it again."
"I'll teleport the machine in when I'm finished. I won't bring the book in again!" Alex offered.

"Ahhh…..why not, it's a useless machine anyway. Just pull that huge plug from that machine and the small one from the wall."

"Thanks boss!" Alex smiled.

"No problem, hey if you fix it, I might give you a raise, a bonus and extended vacation." The boss smiled to Alex.

"Wow, thanks!" Alex grinned.

After unplugging the machine, Alex teleported the machine to his house in the village of Ferlock. In actuality Alex would only have two days to work on the machine. He was going with his wife and son on a holiday to Hawaii. (Strange that this dimension can have places and countries similar to the real world eh?)

Going back to Alex asking Norman to look after his house, Norman had popped over to water Alex's plants. When going to the front door, he noticed Ralph O'Ryan the anthropomorphic sheep there. Ralph was Norman's neighbour. He was wearing his black top hat like always.

"Ralph? What are you doing here?" Norman asked.

"I lent Alex a book of mine and I want it back, but he doesn't seem to be in." Ralph replied.

"Alex is on holiday. He assigned me to look after his house." Norman told Ralph.

"Oh…..do you think I could come in and get it back?"

"Fine." Norman frowned.

Norman and Ralph entered Alex's house. Ralph looked around Alex's living room. It was neat, tidy and was decorated with football posters.

"Wow, such a neat place, whoa! When did he get that big T.V! You think I could watch the football game here?"

Norman thought it over. "Ugh……fine." He said resigned.

"I'll try not to make a mess." Ralph smiled.

"Hey, make all the mess you want, he asked me to look after his house and he knows my low standards."

Ralph frowned. "Ah yes…….no nudy magazines around in this place."
Ralph then smiled. "Hey, I can help you water the plants if you like?"

"Fine, grab a watering can, two are in the kitchen."

Norman noticed that his book of magic sat on top of the machine with the scepter turned on. Alex had not turned it off. He watered the plants a short distance from the machine. He then sat the watering can down and looked at the machine. Ralph came in to make sure he hadn't forgotten any duties. He then noticed the machine. "What's this thing?" Ralph asked Norman.

"Well according to what Alex tells me. This is from his job at WASA and it's a machine for detecting aliens from other planets." Norman told Alex without taking his eyes off the machine.

Ralph was amazed. "Wow." He said.

Norman blew a raspberry with his tongue and frowned. "What a useless machine. Even it aliens and UFO's existed, what makes you think they'd even tolerate the satellite spying on them? If UFO's existed. They'd probably shoot it with a laser. And come on 1597 Clastonia years and this is the best they can do? The way technology is these days they could probably build a much more bigger machine and not just teleport aliens from other planets but other dimensions! Plus information on the species and where it came from!"

Suddenly a loud explosion appeared and both Ralph and Norman shook in shock, the scepter had overheard the conversation and upon hearing "Teleport" it granted Norman's wish. A purple glow appeared all around the machine and it started to grow, computer screens then got added to the machine. More switches then started to appear.

"Whoa!" Ralph and Norman said together.

Ralph and Norman stared at the machine. "Will it……work?" Ralph said shocked.

"Doubt it, it's not plugged in. But I can generate electricity for it."

Norman took his scepter and magic book and pointed it at the machine. "Temporary electricity power up. 30 minutes!" he yelled. He then turned the machine on.

"Greetings I am Boltson the talking alien teleporter. How may I help you?"

"Are we REALLY doing this?" Ralph asked nervouslly.

"This is our chance to meet aliens! Of course we're doing this!" Norman grinned.

"But what if the alien is dangerous!"

"I can program to teleport the most harmless, helpless creature." The computer responded.

"Alright then. Do that and let's go with teleporting aliens from other dimensions. The old machine hadn't detected aliens for more than 50 years straight!" decided Norman.

Loud buzzing and clanking noises were made. Norman and Ralph were afraid the machine was going to blow up. But finally the noise quieted down and baby noises were made from what looked a locker door.

Norman opened the door. It was a baby human crying his eyes out.

Norman was a little disappointed. "A human? They're rare but they already exist in this dimension."

Ralph seemed a little nervous. "Uh-oh, want if we've kidnapped someone's human baby in THIS dimension!?"

"No." the computer responded. This is a male human baby from a dimension called Earth, he appears to be from an orphanage in Scotland.

"Orphanage? Aww...poor baby."

"Well we've got no need for him here. Let's send him back." Norman pointed to the locker.

"No, I'll take care of him." Ralph lifted the baby.

Norman lifted an eyebrow. "What......you're going to become this child's dad?"

"Yeh...." Ralph replied. "You heard the machine, he's harmless."

Norman thought it over. "I.......I got nothing. He's yours." He answered and then turned the machine off. Well that's enough weirdness for today.

Ralph turned to the machine. "How do we explain the machine to Alex?"

"Oh, don't worry about that. He then pointed the scepter to the machine and said. "Time period for objects, take this machine back half an hour."

At this the machine turned back into the machine it once was. It was as if nothing had happened to it.

"Handy spell, wonder why Alex couldn't use it to fix the machine?" asked Ralph.

"Oh...it only goes back an hour and can only be used once every 6 months."

"What kind of magic is that?" Ralph asked.

"You think I make the rules on how these spells are written in the books!?" Norman snarled. "Why is Cinderella only allowed magic till midnight yet Sleeping Beauty sleeps forever till a kiss from a prince!?"

"Alright, chill yourself out."

The baby was named Dougal McKenzall O'Ryan. Well originally the baby was named Dougal McKenzall according to the name tag given on the jacket from his previous owners. But Ralph still kept his name adding his own surname.

CHAPTER FOUR

Snork and Snerk pursue Amy's magic book

Present day Clastonia, 1622.

After saving the city of Sunchester from Phobix's destruction. Amy the elf had become a hero and sort of a minor celebrity. She had been interviewed by a newspaper and when interviewed, some interesting facts came about her, nothing too personal as she provided the answers.

Amy and her sister Misty had come from a long line of elf magician ancestors. They were the ancestors of Colin Woolruffe. Colin had duplicated his magic book at least five times, and over the more than 800 years in his general shop in Ferlock, the magic books had all evolved into very powerful books. Not as destructive as Phobix's dark magic though.

Now you might ask how a small village general store could stay in business for more than 800 years. But don't forget, there are magic blocks that randomly appear and produce gold coins, plus Colin had the power to duplicate gold coins whether they wanted. In Clastonia, people seemed to do jobs more as hobbies and not just to get money.

Plus Colin once did manage to sell one of his duplicate magic books for one million gold coins. When asked where he got the money to buy the book. He just got a snarled. "None of your business!" Before leaving the store.

Over generation after generation, the Woolruffe elf family had looked after the general store. All promised to use their magic only for good. Many of them married other elves and they were worried over the greed that other species might see in the book. It seemed slightly racist or speciest. But it was better that, then another Phobix in the family.

Not all the Woolruffes had taken care of the store, many had moved to get jobs in other areas, but there was always at least one Woolruffe to take care of the store. This was to try and keep their magic in one place and to keep it from spreading and falling in the wrong hands.

The present day Woolruffes, were father Gerald Woolruffe, and his twin daughters, Amy and Misty Woolruffe. Who is their mother? Well, that's a mystery for now.

Gerald and Misty had taken care of the general store, but Amy was different, she wanted to see jobs in other areas, so by permission she had received the ability to work in a library in the city of Sunchester.

When asked by the newspaper what gave her the heart to save her city. Amy just replied.

"Well, I wasn't about to go and look for another job."

After the incident. Amy had been allowed a week off to relax and to make sure the monsters didn't try anything again. If anything happened she could read the undo spell again.

After a week's holiday and no disruption from the monsters, Amy talked to the boss about letting her back, and the boss agreed.

One morning she said goodbye to her sister at her home.

"You're going to work!? Are you nuts?" asked a frantic Misty.

"Misty, I'm a powerful sorceress. I fear nothing. It may be that over 800 years ago. Women sat down got butt raped and didn't fight back. But this is 1622! And magic isn't the only thing evolved! Women have too!"

"You always were brave. You're just like what Dad said about Mum." Misty smiled. "I won't stop you."

On her way to borrow her father's car. She decided to ask her father Gerald for another magic book.
"Why?" Gerald asked.

"Let's say if the monsters get my book, they'll be hell to pay with the spare." Amy grinned.

"Oh, OKAY!" Gerald smiled back.

After getting the second best magic book. Amy set out to work in her red car, after reaching the city of Sunchester. Snork von Snaffler stood behind a dumpster in an alley watching her. He grinned and pulled a mobile phone out of his denim shorts.

"Snerk." He smiled. "Amy Woolruffe just entered the library."

Suddenly the doors on the dumpster behind Snork burst open and Snerk appeared.

"Let's go!" he grinned devilishly.

Snork frowned. "What were you doing in that dumpster!?"

"Can you believe somebody threw out twelve issues of this cooking magazine?"

Snork facepalmed. "Just shut up and get in the library! You got the books of magic?"

"You bet I do!"

Snork and Snerk went over to the library desk where Amy worked. They pointed their scepters at her.

"Hand over your book of magic!" Snork yelled at Amy.

Amy pretended to be scared as she got her small book of magic out and handed it to Snork.

"Nice move, toots." Grinned Snerk.

Snork and Snerk turned to leave. As they got out to leave, as they got out the front door, Amy got out her spare book of magic.

"Fish Carcass those two monsters and lots of it." Amy said to the scepter.

As Snork and Snerk got out the library, a huge dark cloud hovered over them. The monster stopped and got confused.

26

Snork stuck his hand out. "Is it about to rain?" he asked. The brothers looked up and screamed in horror.

A huge pile of dead fish fell on top of the brothers.

Amy then spoke to the scepter. "Teleport my stolen book to me! And teleport those two monsters back to where they came!"

The monsters teleported back to Deathstar to where they came.

After teleporting just outside the city, Snerk then sniffed Snork and said to him.

"And I thought you smelled bad the first time." He groaned.

Amy pointed the scepter at her book. "CLEAN MAGIC BOOK!" and removed the fishy smell off her stolen book.

But Amy wasn't yet finished. She went outside to the huge pile of dead fish.

"Teleport these dead fishes to the nearest dump!" She yelled to her scepter.

Unfortunately the scepter had misunderstood Amy's command. The dead fishes ended up outside Norman the goblin's sloppy untidy house.

"What kind of cruel joke is this!?" Norman yelled.

Chapter 5

Snork and Snerk pursue Amy's magic book. TAKE TWO!

The next day, Amy went to her job at the library again. She sat down and started reading a book. (Not a magic one.) When Snork and Snerk walked over to her, not carrying magic books, but revolvers. Amy looked up and saw the monsters. Her eyes sunk.

"You again." She sighed.

"Yes, us again." Snerk smiled.

"You don't learn your lesson, do you?" She asked without hesitating.

"We learned something, we'll use revolvers instead of books." Snork replied simply.

"What's the difference?" Amy asked.

"Time has to be wasted turning to pages and reading words, but not with revolvers. You press the button and BOOM! You're dead!" Snerk laughed manically.

"Pokémon's Team Rocket is more competent than you." Amy groaned.

"I'd watch the talk lady, or you'll end up with a bullet in your face!" Snork cocked his gun.

Snerk looked around. "Hey Snork, you think we could kill everybody in this library? Show the people here not to mess with the monsters!"

Some citizens ducked under tables. Amy's eyes widened a little in fright.

Snork turned to Snerk "Snerk, we can't just kill loads of innocent people." He scolded. "A huge massacre by monsters would possibly lead to another war being declared on Deathstar and is that really what you want!? You really are insane."

Amy gave a sigh of relief.

"I want some SENSELESS VIOLENCE!" Snerk moaned loudly.

Snork turned back to Amy "I'll get you a puppy to torture later. Let's not lose track of our mission. Hand over all the books of magic you have! In fact tell us where your store is, so we can have ALL the books you have!"

"No need, here they ALL are." Amy got out her backpack and emptied out five books of magic onto the counter. Snork and Snerk stared at the books in awe.

"Wise decision." Snork smiled. "When we rule the world, we'll save you a spot in our top military ranks."

"C'mon, let's get outta here before the cops come." Snork and Snerk ran out the library.

A citizen who was an anthropomorphic female gazelle walked up to Amy. "Aren't you afraid of what's going to happen with those books!?" She said panicked.

Amy turned to the shook up citizen. "Don't panic ma'am. I've got it all under control."

"Why don't you call the police!?" she yelled.

Amy kept calm. "Just give it twenty minutes. Besides when it comes to magic, I don't even think the military can handle this kind of thing. Repeat. Twenty minutes."

"What's going to happen in twenty minutes!?" the gazelle citizen yelled.

"Stick around and find out." Amy smiled back to her calmly. "I assure you, everything's fine."

The gazelle citizen now seemed sure of Amy's plan. "Okay. I trust you." She said slowly.

Twenty minutes passed. Amy then picked up the phone and dialled the number for the general store her sister and father worked in. Misty answered the phone. "Hello?" she answered.

"Misty, it's Amy, get the one book of magic the monsters didn't get and teleport the books back."

"You got it, sis."

Meanwhile at the city of Deathstar in Phobix's huge castle, Phobix was surprised to see Snork and Snerk in the throne room where she sat with the books of magic.

Phobix was amazed. "You did it. YOU DID IT ! ! The books are ours! The WORLD IS MINE ! ! "

"Don't you mean ours?" asked Snork.

"Oh yes, of course." Phobix took one of the books and began to scan the first page. But before she could read the third word of the first page. The book disappeared out of her hand, along with the other Woolruffe magic books. Phobix was furious. Snork and Snerk opened their mouths in shock.

Phobix's eyes spat hate at Snork and Snerk. "Didn't I tell you what would happen if I experienced more failure?" she snarled.

"We have a very, very, cunning elf on our hands." Snerk said to Snork.

"Miss, it's not our fault!" pleaded a terrified Snork.

Phobix grabbed her own magic book. "TORTURE TIME!" she yelled.

What happens next is a little too violent. Let's just say it involved big spikes and a lot of fire, did the Von Snaffler brothers die? Well no......Phobix is actually capable of restoring life. But let's say the brothers did meet a lot of pain before they died, and Phobix brought them back because she couldn't be bothered to make new friends.

Chapter 6

Did you notice that in the last chapter Amy was completely fearless? But have you wondered why and how Amy managed to stay so calm. Even before the catastrophic incident with Sunchester, Amy and her sister Misty had always used their magic powers for the good of folk.
    Word got out on their magic however and people cruel and kind wanted to use their magic.

In the city of Sunchester, Amy and Misty had just finished watching a movie in the cinema. It was 11pm when the movie had finished and the sisters had gone to the bus station to get a bus back to Ferlock.

"That was a great movie." Misty said to Amy.

"That murderer was terrifying and how'd they make the blood look so real?" Amy said a little frightened.

"Man you should've seen your hair shoot up when we got that jumpscare. You looked like a blonde haired, Marge Simpson!"

"Ugh…..Good thing I brought my comb. I will not look like an overused and past its prime cartoon character." She frowned.

When they got to the Sunchester city bus station, there were almost no buses there and very few staff were around. They went to the spot where they usually got a bus.

Misty read a bus timetable.

"Next bus is in ten minutes." She told Amy.

"You wanna get a taxi?" Amy asked.

"Nah…..I can wait."

"The fish and chip shop is still open. You wanna………" Amy didn't finish as a huge dark shadow covered them. Both sisters turned to see a blue troll. The troll was almost twice the size of Amy. Muscular with huge arms, wore a red sweater with black stripes and brown shorts. He had purple hair.

"Hello girls? Are you by any chance Amy and Misty Woolruffe?" he asked.

"Who wants to know." Misty snarled. "Give some warning before you sneak up on people! You gave us a fright!"

"ARE YOU OR AREN'T YOU AMY AND MISTY WOOLRUFFE!?" he yelled at them. Misty backed down scared.

"Yes we are. What of it?" Amy asked.

"I'm heard of you girls and your magic. I've come a long way to talk to you. My wife along with many is dying from a horrible illness. Come with me and cure her illness. I come from a small town of trolls, a ten hour journey that way.

"Ten hours….FORGET IT!" Misty snapped.

Amy turned to Misty and held up an index finger. "Now….now……that is no way to speak to our guest."

"Sorry….I'm tired and I'm cranky. It's past my bedtime." Misty moaned.

Amy turned back to the troll. "We'd love to help you and we're sorry to hear about your wife, but none of our spells can cure deadly disease."

The troll looked disappointed. "Can you bring the dead back to life?"

"Ooooo…..sorry." Misty shrugged. "You might want to try Merloch the magician. He lives in Benthrope, a city four hours that way. Misty pointed west.

"He removed every AIDS related disease from this rabbit prostitute. And now she's the best looking prostitute again!" Misty offered.

"If you take the right shortcuts, you might make it to Benthorpe in three." Amy pointed to the west with Misty with her finger.

The troll thought it over and got angry. "You girls are lying to avoid work! I'm taking you anyway!" At this he removed a huge metal pipe he'd kept hidden in the sleeve of his jumper.

"Shall we tell him how hardass we really are?" Misty asked Amy.

"Let him find out." Amy smiled.

The troll slammed the pipe down on Amy's head. Suddenly the troll shook as if somebody had hit HIM in the face with a pipe. Amy and Misty jumped out of the way as the troll crashed onto the pavement.

"Good job with that 24 hour reflect spell before we left the house." Amy smiled to Misty. She gave a thumbs up to Misty and Misty thumbed up back.

The loud crash had alerted a security guard. He was a tall skinny human with a moustache "What was that noise? Are you girls alright?"

"We're fine." Misty smiled but call the cops and tell them to bring an extra large pair of handcuffs.

"And a lot of deodorant." Amy added.

Chapter 7

Amy and Misty lived together in a flat where they paid the bills half among themselves. They visited their father often. One night after work, Amy decided to spend some time with Dougal playing video games. She visited her father's home to get some video games.

She walked into her father's home to see Gerald and Misty with sleeping bags and packing a few things into a suitcase.

"What's all this?" Amy asked her dad.

"Amy, get packed, we're going to spend a night in the general store." Gerald turned to Amy.

"Why, is this some sort of silly holiday?" she joked.

"No, those monsters might try to steal the books in the store."

"With us around. They'll be no match!" Misty grinned.

"You're being a little paranoid, aren't you?" she asked. "The monsters don't know where the general store is."

"They know we live in Ferlock if they read that newspaper report. Ferlock is only a small village, and we're only one of A FEW general stores!"

"Well you can go do that, I'm going to hang out with Dougal." Amy said to Gerald.

"Well I suppose we can hold the store without you. Stay safe." Gerald replied.

"Oh....you gonna go hang out with your boyfriend?" Misty teased.

"Dougal and I are just friends." Amy frowned.

"Of course you are." Gerald smiled.

Amy folded her arms in stern. "Why is that so hard to believe?"

"You two have so much in common." Gerald replied.

"Yeh....you're both giant nerds, you both wear glasses, love science-fiction, play video games and you've been friends since primary school. Why DO YOU believe you're not boyfriend and girlfriend?"

Amy sighed. "Alright fine.....Dougal's a nice guy but he's kinda wimpish."

Misty shrugged. "Not his fault, he has no experience with magic and was one of the few humans in school. You were one of his few friends along with that dragon of his that protected him from bullies."

Amy continued. "Plus I won't lie, I have tried to be appealing to him but he's always had a very low sex drive. He's told us before he's asexual you know. One time I got his mail and tried to deliver it wearing a T-shirt with half the bottom missing and a very short skirt. You wanna know the only thing he said?"

"What's that?" Misty asked smiling.

"Thank you very much. Took the mail and closed the door."

"How inconsiderate!" Misty frowned.

"No, not entirely. He did open the door again and offered something."

"What's that?" Misty asked.

"Do you want a jacket? It's kinda cold out. He said to me."

Misty chuckled. "How sweet of him. He MUST have a sex drive. He surely must. He'd be grumpy and angry with testosterone if he didn't."

"Anyway We're just gonna go play video games. No biggie." Finished Amy.

"Naughty X-rated video games?" Gerald asked smiling.

"NO!"

"We're just teasing, because we love you honey. Have a nice night." Gerald replied.

"Right, thanks." Amy got the stuff she needed and went to Dougal's home which was a rented flat.

Dougal worked at the supermarket Wesco for only 16 hours a week. Not like Amy who worked 25 hours a week in the library. He had a general short attention span and loved having fun mostly playing video games. He didn't have very many friends and was shy, but it didn't bother him. He had difficulty paying attention in school and had to have somebody sit beside him to help him pay attention.

Dougal was diagnosed with Asperger's Syndrome. But despite having a hidden disability it didn't let him get it down. What's odd was that for most of his young life, he was unaware he had it. He found out only in the last years of secondary school, he was disabled, he came across a bunch of sheets in a drawer entitled, "Does your child has Asperger's Syndrome?" that had been given to Ralph in a school meeting. And as he read the sheets......much of the behaviour actually matched his."

"Holy crap." Dougal thought to himself. "I'm disabled."

Dougal didn't have the best social skills, but they were a few people he trusted. Amy, Misty, Thorak and Garrett, all close friends to him.

Amy knocked on Dougal's door and Dougal answered. "Hey Amy, come on in."

Amy entered Dougal's flat. There were many video game posters around but not a single nudie poster in sight.

"Asexual." Amy thought.

Amy and Dougal played video games a few hours into the night. And even watched a few episodes of a sitcom while eating popcorn together. Around midnight, Amy yawned.

"Well it's late. Wanna call it a night?" asked Dougal.

"Sure thing. You want me to stay the night?" Amy offered.

"There's only one bed, you want me to sleep on the couch?" Dougal asked.

"No…..I was thinking we could share it." Amy offered a little nervously.

"Isn't that what people in love do?" Dougal asked smiling.

Amy held up her hands. "Not necessary, me and Misty have shared a bed before."

Dougal smiled. "Look Amy, you seem a nice girl, but you're not my type."

"How come?" Amy asked.

Dougal thought it over and answered "Well for starters I don't have a lot of ambition in my life. You want to achieve a high career, me I'm perfectly fine with just being a customer assistant. I enjoy having fun and having a lot of fun to do it. I probably could search for a higher job but I'd get bored with it."

"Well don't you have any dreams?" asked Amy.

"I do, but they're pretty unserious, I always wanted to be a cartoonist or a book author. But for being a cartoonist. I sucked at telling jokes. My dad and Thorak will probably tell you how bad I sucked at telling jokes. As for books, I once tried to get a book published but they turned it down everywhere I went. And eventually even I myself thought the story wasn't that good. I want to tell a story and get it published but I regularly suffer from writer's block."

"I see." Amy replied.

"Well that, and I can't stand the idea of having kids. Kids are immature little brats who want chocolate every time you enter a supermarket. I don't think I'd make a good dad."

"Oh….." Amy looked down.

Dougal comforted Amy. "I do care for you Amy, but in a different way."

"I care for you too." Amy replied. "Can I at least give you a kiss on the cheek for a good night?" Amy smiled.

"I suppose." Dougal smiled.

Amy kissed Dougal on the cheek and they waved goodbye to each other.

Chapter 8
Spell gone wrong

In the monster city of Deathstar, Phobix had been attempting to get back at Amy herself for constantly foiling her plans. She had attempted a nasty spell that would have made her have horrible flatulence for one day. Unfortunately it hadn't gone well……as Amy had been wearing a reflect spell, the spell had ended upon her. So Phobix had sat in her throne with some bad gas. While sulking and swearing to herself.

"Curse that fucking elf." Phobix swore as she let out a huge ripper. "Damnit……I think my red dress got even more brown."

Snork entered wearing a peg over his nose. "Hey, queen." He greeted smiling. Even he thought Phobix's spell backfiring was funny.

"Hey…." She said in a huff.

"I know you're down, but I know what'll cheer you up!" Snork raised his voice. He had to do this over the long farting Phobix was doing.

"Damnit…….I smell like refried ass ten times over! What could possibly help!?" Phobix yelled

"How about a juggling act. Aarot the jester has just picked up a nice new juggling act." Snork offered.

"Oh what the hell….gonna do something to pass this crummy day. Send him in."

Aarot appeared wearing a gas mask he was a short green monster with three eyes sticking up out of his head in long sockets. Luckily he still had a nose and ears and a face so he could wear the gas mask. He had four arms and wore a jester outfit.

"Greetings Phobix, I've been working on a dangerous jugging act, I've wrapped rags to the end of these bowling pins and doused them in petrol." He took out a lighter. "I'll just light them on fire and…."

"NO!" Phobix screamed interrupting.

KABOOM ! ! !

From all of Phobix's flatulence, the room exploded, glass windows smashed as Phobix was thrown into the back wall. Snork and Aarot laid on the ground injured. Bookcases had thrown over and furniture was ruined. Phobix's throne room was a wreck.
Snork weakly got up. He walked over to Phobix slowly now with holes in her red dress and burn marks in her clothes. She had her eyes closed and looked unconscious.

"Queen? You okay…….." Snork asked. Instead of a voice. He got a nice long fart instead.

Aarot joined Snork dizzy. "Yeh…..she's okay."

Phobix opened her eyes and stared at Snork and Aarot.

"Think we better get outta here." Gulped Snork.

As they ran out the room. Phobix screamed.

"YOU TWO GET OUTTA HERE BEFORE I CRAP MY PANTS!!!"

Chapter 9

A short chapter featuring Dougal and Thorak!

Dougal and Thorak had decided to go fishing the other day. They were in a huge lake near the forest. Dougal was enjoying the fresh air but Thorak looked nervous.

"Are you sure there are no creature other than fish that live in this lake." He asked Dougal nervously.

"Yep." Dougal replied back.

"No sea monsters?" Thorak asked.

"No, it's a great lake and plenty of people fish here. Why are you so nervous?"

"You wanna hear the tale of the last time I went fishing?" Thorak frowned.

LAST TIME.

Thorak was fishing in another lake when he got a bite.

"Yeep." Thorak jumped in excitement. He kept tugging and tried to pull the fish in, it was a heavy one!

Thorak pulled his catch out of the water. It was a muscular merman and he did not look happy!

Thorak's long ears dropped in fright. "Uh oh!" gulped Thorak.

The merman punched Thorak in the face giving him a black eye and knocking him unconscious. The merman then jumped back into the water.

PRESENT.

"Oh yeah." Dougal smiled. "We had to put a frozen steak on your eye."

"It's not funny!" Thorak snarled.

Chapter 10
Spying

While Phobix's throne room was being redecorated. Phobix spoke to Snork and Snerk outside her castle.

"Alright major morons, new plan. You two are going to spy on Amy the whole day and work out her weakness and report any you find!" Phobix barked to Snork and Snerk.

"Spy on her the whole day? How?" Snerk frowned.

"Simple. Invisibilty!" Phobix answered.

"You can do that?" asked Snork.

Phobix got her magic book and pointed her scepter at Snork and Snerk.

"Magic! Make these monsters invisible!" Phobix yelled.

At this Snork and Snerk became invisible.

"Neat!" grinned Snerk.

"Awesome!" smiled Snork.

"Remember, do not hurt Amy in anyway! At least for now. Find out any weaknesses and report back to me."

"With how powerful she is. I highly doubt we can do that." Snerk responded.

"What will you be doing?" asked Snork.

"Me? For starters I'm going to get some new furniture destroyed by my bad gas." Phobix snarled.

Snork and Snerk started to laugh.

"Not funny! Magic, Teleport these monsters to the city Sunchester! Outside Sunchester library!"

Snork and Snerk teleported away to the Sunchester library.

"Why can't she just do that to get Amy's magic books?" Snerk growled.

"She's tried that. The books have some sort of anti teleport system on them and the teleport spells can only be carried out by the person who cast the spell on the books. There's also a way that the anti teleport magic book spell can be moved onto other books of magic and that the teleport book spell can be cast only by certain books."

"Really?" Snerk asked Snork.

"Yep, damn elf thought of everything. Well let's go in……"

The monsters went into the library. Amy sat at her desk reading a book. (Again not a magic one.) Snork and Snerk sat behind Amy's desk waiting for something to happen.

"This is boring." Snerk whispered to Snork. "Are we really supposed to just sit around all day for something to happen." Snerk then yawned.

The yawn surprised Amy a little. She looked around to see where the noise was coming from.

"Keep it down." Snork whispered to Snerk snarling.

Suddenly a loud voice appeared on a speaker. "Amy Woolruffe. Please come to my office."

"The boss?" Amy thought. "Why does he wanna see me?"

Amy got up and went to go see her boss. She took her handbag which contained her magic book.

"Rats." Thought Snork.

Amy's boss was an overweight short anthropomorphic pig who wore a shirt and a tie. He went by the name of Nathan Nelson.

Amy entered the room of her boss. Snork and Snerk had attempted to follow Amy but had ended up getting the door slammed on their faces. After rubbing their faces in pain. They then decided to listen through the door.

Nathan pointed to a chair. "Have a seat." He said.

"I've already got one at home." Amy joked.

Nathan wasn't pleased at Amy's joke. "Just sit." He said in a gruff. Nathan held his hands together "Amy, do you know why I called you here?"

"To congratulate me on my hard work?" Amy smiled.

"No! You've been bringing magic to work, and I'm not happy with it." He said in a huff.

"I'm only trying to defend myself." Amy frowned.

"True, but your magic isn't looking good to anyone. People are complaining that they are getting strong smells of fish near the entrance. And they have been terrified to come to the library."

Amy began to get annoyed. "They're terrified because of terrorist monsters! Let's go with what you're saying, are you saying I leave the book at home and get kidnapped, shot dead or something worse!? One of them even suggested shooting dead everybody in the library!"

"I still haven't got my satisfaction of violence." Snerk frowned outside the door.

Snork hit Snerk on the head. "Shut up!"

Nathan thought it over and got frightened. "Uh…….really?"

"YES!" Amy yelled.

"I'm still sick of all this chaos." Nathan sighed.

"You should be thankful, a short time ago, this was all a bunch of rubble caused by meteors. I undid it!" Amy shouted.

"Ah….did I mention that being squashed by a meteor is surprisingly painless?" Nathan said to Amy.

"No you did not." Amy replied.

"Look can't you find at least a less destructive way to get rid of your enemies? The reason I haven't talked to you sooner is because I'm somewhat scared of you."

Amy began to back down. "Really?"

"But you seem a nice girl out for truth and justice, and I worked up the courage to talk to you." Nathan said in a scared voice.

Amy began to sympathize with Nathan. "Look tell you what. How about the next time the monsters attack, I'll stop them in a way which involves the police and the monsters will be put in jail. After that I'll stop bringing my book in, okay?"

Nathan thought it over. "Well……alright……" he said after a few seconds.

"Hell, tell you what give it one week, if the monsters stop attacking this area after a week. I'll stop bringing my magic book in."

Nathan thought it over. "That's……good too."

Amy smiled at Nathan to convince him with the deal.

"Thank you for listening to me and not hurting me in any way." Nathan smiled.

"Evil doesn't please me." Amy smiled as she stood up and went back to her job.

Before she went back to her desk, she decided to use the toilet. Snork and Snerk continued to follow.

"Hmmm…….feeling bored were you, Snerk? Let's go in and see her take a dump." Snork grinned to Snerk.

Amy went to a bathroom stall and sat down on the toilet. Snork and Snerk entered the stalls beside her. Snork on the left and Snerk on the right.

"She may be on the side of good but she's a babe." Snork thought watching Amy do her business.

Amy started to hear chuckles and began to get suspicious. She got out her magic book. She then turned to the page and found a spell that could cancel all spells cast on a person in a small area.

"Cancel all spells in this area!" she spoke to her scepter.

At this Snork and Snerk began to become visible. Amy looked around to see Snork and Snerk looking at her.

"Why you dirty perverts!" she yelled angrily.

"Uh-oh." Gulped Snork.

"Teleport monsters to front of stall!" she yelled to her scepter.

Amy stood up, pulled up her skirt and opened the door to see a scared Snork and Snerk.

"Double slap these monsters! Two hands!" Amy yelled to her scepter.

At this two white hands appeared in mid air and slapped Snork and Snerk.

"Teleport these monsters back to where they came!" Amy yelled to her scepter.

Snork and Snerk teleported back to Deathstar where they came. But Amy didn't teleport them to prison.

The reason? She liked a challenge. That and Phobix probably would have teleported them out of prison.

"I'm an evolved woman." She thought. "No sitting and getting butt raped for me." She smiled.

Chapter 11
Incompetent evil ruler

In her now newly decorated throne room. Phobix sat in her throne room. She had heard that Snork and Snerk had failed on their mission.

"Incompetent morons." Phobix face palmed.

Snerk frowned. "Oh………come on. Hasn't Amy shown to you by now, she's a very powerful sorceress? Give it up!"

"Never!" Phobix slammed her hands on the table.

"Well in the meantime, you want to hear how our soldiers have been doing?" asked Snork.

Phobix was the ruler of her army. Although she had many generals such as Snork and Snerk themselves, she did give orders to her military, from time to time. Phobix's army consisted mainly of monsters who wielded guns and not books of magic. She did however award books of magic to anyone who pleased her making them very powerful soldiers. She had never considered robots like the other countries as it was too expensive and she thought dark magic was way better.

Surprisingly despite Phobix's evil, the soldiers had carried out peace keeping missions, eliminating poor countries from terrorists. In Clastonia poor countries did exist, they existed poor countries where magic for some reason wasn't all that common. Magic had never made it to countries tons of miles away. And issues like poverty and difficulty growing food were common. This of course led to crime. Phobix had actually had terrorists eliminated. However she believed that only she should be allowed to terrorize and had actually had her soldiers try to get the terrorists over to her side. If they didn't take the offer they were shot dead. Very few people ever joined.

"Ahh…..the mission in Sathtopia. How have they being doing?" asked Phobix.

"Pretty good." Snork responded.

"Any joining survivors?" Phobix asked.

"None." Snork said simply.

"Damnit! Why doesn't anybody ever join!? Don't they want to learn evil dark magic?" Phobix snapped.

"According to what I hear, their evil has standards." Snork responded.

"What!?" Phobix yelled.

"While they do commit crimes they do it so they can continue living. They're not interested in massive destruction for the sake of massive destruction."

Phobix closed her eyes. "Unbelievable…..I'm so evil, I come across terrorists with a conscience."

Snork shrugged.

Phobix opened her eyes. "Well I'll show them! Tell me more Sathtopia."

Snork thought the country over. "Well it's a country of only around a million located in Africa. The literacy rate is only 40 percent. It's populated by both talking and non-talking warthogs, antelope, hyenas, cheetahs, widebeast and all kinds of African style animals. It's so poor that the talking animals eat the other talking animals as well as the non-talking animals. Many of the areas go through power outages around 16 to 20 hours a day. The president was disposed a few years ago by a military coup and is run by General Palkins , who is also a warthog general in the military. He's grown rather hated in recent years."

"Hated?" Phobix asked. "How come?"

"Well you know how in all the commercials for Sathtopia, donations in money can be given to the country?" Snork asked.

"As a rule, he made he has to look over the money donations and decide what to do with the money. He's been treating himself to many luxury items with the money. And usually uses very little money to build schools and hospitals and has been using the money to build swimming pools for himself and his military buddies, additions to his mansion, building unnecessary buildings such as discos and tattoo parlours. The list is endless." Continued Snork.

"Wow, what a douche." Frowned Snerk.

"I always did have him down for a dumbass." Phobix frowned.

"Oh, he is." Snork continued in the frowning.

Phobix thought over everything Snork had said. "Hmmm…..only a million citizens? In the whole of the country Monstropolis, my city has more citizens than him, If you're going to conquer the world might as well start slow. Forget about Amy for now.

Meanwhile in Sathtopia, General Zane Palkins was relaxing in a jacuzzi in his mansion where the swimming pool was. When his cheetah secretary Isabis walked up to him.

"Hey, cutie." He smiled. "Any news?"

"Well, the letter bombs you've been receiving have been increasing and now even some of your men now hate you for opening the letter bomb letters for you. And that hate you've been receiving has increased due to the protesters you've had executed outside your mansion. Many people have started protesting all over the country against you." Isabis responded. "And it looks higher than the number of military personnel you have."

"My god……I really messed up bad." Zane looked down.

Isabis shook her head. "It's not looking good."

Phobix then teleported in front of Zane and Isabis.

"Greetings, General Palkins." She smiled.

"Who the hell are you?" shouted Zane.

"I'm here to kick your butt and take your country." Grinned Phobix. "Will there be war or…"

"Oh, THANK YOU! THANK YOU!" Zane beamed in excitement.

"Wait what?" Phobix got confused.

"Everybody hates me! My country is all yours! Just do me a favour." General Palkins begged.

"What's that?" Phobix asked.

"Get me a home in your country! Away from here!"

"Sure thing."

Phobix took over Sathtopia easily, with the high level of gold coins she had from her country Monstropolis, she transformed the poor country into a somewhat stable country and opened up many schools and educational facilities. And gained much respect for it. Much of Palkins' troops joined hers.

Phobix had kept her promise. Palkins had gained his own home in Monstropolis and even gained a magic book from Phobix for being so cooperative. He and his previous secretary Isabis moved in together.

"Even though Phobix gained much respect. She felt somewhat disappointed that she also wasn't feared."

"Nuts." She thought. "Even when I win. I lose."

Some of you might have thought this chapter pointless. But it does serve a point later on.

Can Amy defeat Phobix forever? Only time will tell. Stay tuned.

Chapter 12

Meanwhile in the village of Ferlock, Amy had been showing Dougal her magic book in his flat, Amy had been considering Dougal trustworthy enough for him to take a look at her spell book and even try out a few spells, the harmless ones of course. Dougal had tried out spells such as making a rainbow appear in both his hands and an odd spell that made a really large roll of toilet paper appear along with three peas.

"Your magic is awesome." Dougal smiled.

"Glad you think so." Amy smiled.

Dougal turned to Amy "Listen there's something I've been wanting to ask you."

"What's that?" Amy asked.

"You know how you've been telling me about those monsters harassing you at work."

"Yeh?"

"Isn't there anything you can do in your spell book to make them leave you alone for good?" asked Dougal.

"I can't murder anyone, Dougal." Amy frowned. "Eventually the monsters will get the message and leave me alone."

"I highly doubt that."

"They will!"

"Amy you've been harassed three times by them. This has to stop." Dougal frowned. "It might be murder. But justifiable murder!"

Amy thought it over. "Look even if I was on their levels of evil. I don't think I have magic powerful enough to defeat them. Plus they have the ability to raise the dead plus the magic books are indestructible."

"You've got to do something. Phobix is looking for war."

"She's what?"

"According to her words in the newspaper. 'She's looking to take over the world, slowly but steady.' She invaded the country Sathtopia, and got the military there on her side. While that country co-operated. The other neighbouring poor countries haven't been so keen on her taking over. They're all terrified she's going to invade and cause chaos. They've increased their defence, and this country has actually been kind to give them some of the military robots as defence. She's crazy and looking for a war Amy, and she's not going to back down."

Amy struggled to take everything Dougal in.

"I'm still only one person, Dougal, I don't have magic that can eliminate hundreds of monsters." Amy responded.

"Regardless. Do what you think is right." Dougal sighed.

Chapter 13

The invasion of Sathtopia had made the world tense. Countries both poor and rich were tense as to what Phobix was planning next. Some time passed and all remained quiet from the monsters.

But only one thing was on Phobix's mind. Kidnapping Amy Woolruffe. Despite the failure of the mission of spying on Amy. She had heard from Snork and Snerk that Amy wasn't allowed to take her magic book into work. And Phobix figured she could use this to her advantage.

When Amy went into work without her magic book. Only five minutes into her job, Snork and Snerk appeared with their magic books.

"Hiya! " Snerk smiled.

"You really are unoriginal terrorists." Amy folded her arms.

"And you're a powerful sorceress who refuses to die, how are we supposed to be?" Snork frowned.

"Do you have some sort of back up plan?" Snerk asked.

"Nope, take me to your leader, I come in peace." Amy said in a robotic style voice.

Snork closed his eyes in disbelief. Snerk facepalmed.

Snork without opening his eyes yelled at his scepter. "Teleport me, Snerk and Amy to Phobix!"

The three teleported to Phobix's throne room at her castle. Phobix was surprised to see that the plan had come through. She pointed to Amy.

"You…..YOU ! ! ! "

"Me." Amy said quietly.

Phobix walked over to Amy "You've been a bother to me for too long. But it all ends here."

"I should have worn a nappy, I've got a brown skirt. I really do." Amy simply said.

"Oh, you will do!" Phobix then proceeded to slap Amy in the face as hard as she could. But to her surprise. Phobix felt the pain and fell over.

"Ow!" she said in pain.

"I've got my 24 hour pain reflect spell on. You can't hurt me." Amy smiled.

"We'll see about that. Lock her up till the spell wears off!" Phobix yelled to Snork and Snerk.

"Very well." Snork said and turned to his scepter. "Scepter…"

Amy interrupted Snork. "Is it okay if I walk to my cell, I'd like to see this place a bit. You have a lovely castle."

"NO!" Snork yelled. "Teleport Amy to the prison!" he yelled to the scepter.

Amy teleported to the prison and remained there only for under three hours, for she had another spell put on her, a teleport spell that worked by time. When midday came, she teleported back to the general store with her sister and father to have lunch. Gerald and Misty were having lunch in the break room.

"Hey." She said.

"Did the monsters strike again?" Gerald asked.

"Yep." Amy replied truthfully. " That prison." She shuddered "I now know what monster B.O smells like."

"Okay. Enough is enough. Quit your job NOW." Gerald got angry.

"What, but I love working in Sunchester!" Amy moaned.

"It's dangerous! I can't bring you back to life if you get killed you know! That's four times you've been harassed! One of these days you'll let your guard down and you'll be dead!"

Silence appeared in the break room for a few seconds. At this Amy sighed. "Hmph.......well maybe you're right."

At that moment, for the first time in fifty years Gerald's oldest magic book that had been sitting on the shelf without an update gave a white glow.

"Hey.....your book gained a new magic spell." Amy pointed to the book.

Gerald opened his book. It was the oldest book, the original found by Colin Woolruffe. When Colin turned to the last page. He read the spell and became amazed.

"Wow….." he said.

"What is it?" Misty asked.

"Amy, your troubles are over." Gerald smiled.

Chapter 14

The next day Phobix sat in a huff. That morning she had gone down to get Amy only to find her missing. She sat in the throne room sulking. Snork and Snerk had joined her that morning.

"How does she do it?" Phobix was almost in tears in how Amy had repeatedly ruined her plans.

"Magic, duh." Snerk said simply.

Phobix got up and gave Snerk a slap. She then sat down.

"Look, maybe some good old fashioned blood lust will cheer you up? Why don't we invade one of Sathtopia's neighbouring countries?" Snork proposed.

Phobix thought it over. "Hyph….maybe. After all when I rule most of the world maybe the biggest army will finally stop her."

"Now you're thinking positive!" Snork smiled.

"I can't allow you to go that." Amy had teleported right outside the throne room to where Phobix was and walked in.

Phobix raised an eyebrow. "What, why are you here?"

"I've come to make you a deal." Amy said in a serious voice.

"What sort of deal?" asked Phobix.

"A one on one magic showdown, you and me, if I lose, my relatives will hand you every magic book I have. One catch, I make the first move."

"You'll just use that reflect move you cheater." Growled Phobix.

"Alright then, no reflect moves." Amy said simply.

"It's a trick queen, she probably cast it before she came here." Snork frowned.

"I really haven't." said Amy.

"Liar!" screamed Phobix.

"I can cast a truth spell to prove I haven't." Amy said keeping her calm.

"You're just making that up." Phobix snarled.

"I'm really not, I'll prove it." Amy started to turn some pages in her spell book.

Phobix held up her hand. "Alright, you tell the truth. Do you have some mass murdering spell up your sleeve?"

"No I don't." Amy said simply.

"Wait, what?" Phobix was almost in laughter.

"I don't have spells that can murder lots of people at once." Amy replied.

Phobix smiled evilly "Well I do……don't you know who you're up against? Even death is no match for me! Even if I was killed don't you know I can bring myself back to life?"

"Fair enough, if I win, you have to become a nice woman." Amy said simply still calm. "Couple of rules, I don't cast a reflect smell, I make the first move and you can cast any spell you want."

"I like!" Phobix smiled. "Let's make this area we fight a little more appropriate. Teleport me, Snork, Snerk and Amy to the gladiator area !"

All four teleported to a roman style fighting arena. It was empty and blood stains were all around the arena.

"Take a look at what I do for entertainment." Phobix introduced. "I have had many monsters fight in my arena. For bloody gory entertainment, I award big cash prizes to the winner and even magic books."

"How barbaric." Amy frowned.

"Don't ever let it be said I'm an unkind lady, sometimes I resurrect the loser. Just so they can face the cruel teasing and laughing from the crowd." Phobix smiled. "Snork, Snerk go sit in the audience seats."

Snork and Snerk then went to go sit down. "You go, queen!" Snerk shouted.

"Let's stand a good distance before we fight each other." Amy said to Phobix.

They did that, they both walked backwards without taking their eyes off each other. After walking a good distance. Amy stopped and after a bit so did Phobix.

"We'll go on five seconds. Ready?" Amy shouted to Phobix.

"Ready." Phobix replied.

Amy began the countdown. "5....4....."

"Mega flamethrower!" Phobix interrupted casting her magic.

At this a huge wide range of flames shot towards Amy. Amy jumped in fright. Phobix had cheated in the fight.

"Super huge temporary shield!" A huge blue see-through shield then appeared right in front of Amy protecting her from the flames. The shield then disappeared.

"You cheater!" Amy yelled.

"Why, thank you, pipsqueak." Phobix grinned. "You really think I'd let someone like you make the first move!?" As Phobix made an attempt to cast another spell. Amy read out the new spell that she had learned.

"Absorb and make nothing!" Amy yelled. Suddenly a white ball beam of light appeared above Amy's head. Amy, Phobix, Snork and Snerk closed their eyes at the brightness. Weird magic noises were made from the ball. 30 seconds passed and neither of the four attempted to open their eyes. The white light surrounded the whole of the city of Deathstar. Many monsters were forced to close their eyes and the weird magic noises appeared in random areas. A full minute passed. And as the white light began to dim, the noises went away. After the noises were gone, Amy, Phobix, Snork and Snerk all opened their eyes.

"What the hell was that!" Phobix yelled to Amy.

"I absorbed the magic all around of Deathstar and made it into nothing. The only way to destroy a magic book." Amy yelled back.

Phobix looked around, her spell book was gone and so was Snork and Snerk's. Deathstar was now powerless, Amy had absorbed magic for miles around and made it into nothing.

At this Phobix went into tears. "No………..no… …………………………… my magic. It's all gone."

"I absorbed the magic of your military too. All gone. All except mine." Amy smiled yelling.

"You win, go ahead, get my death over with." Phobix said in a sad tone she had never used before. Amy walked over to Phobix, sobbing madly and on the floor. She had walked over because she was tried of shouting to her.

"I'm not killing you." Amy continued to smile.

"Why not." Phobix asked in tears.

"I refuse to murder and sink to your level. Teleport me away." She teleported away from the arena.

END OF CHAPTER 14
*

Final Chapter of Book 1

When word got out that most of Phobix's army was now powerless. A nasty attack had happened. The robots from Amy's home country attacked leading to the entire annihilation of the city of Deathstar. The orders were simple, kill everybody in Deathstar.

There was never an order to surrender from the queen herself, or an order to fight to the last monster. Phobix, Snork and Snerk had killed themselves from the weapons from the arena. The shock was indescribable to the monster people. Many both normal citizens and soldiers had killed themselves before the robots came.

Generals begged for mercy. But mercy never came. The monsters had repeated wars over and over many times in the past. And upon hearing how powerless every monster was they were going to take every opportunity they had.

Amy herself grew shocked at how big a massacre zone Deathstar became. Many monsters innocent or not, were sent to their deaths.

"I had to do it." She thought one day in her home. "Or else the world would have repeated torture. I would have been repeatedly harassed. It was them or me."

Upon the annihilation of Deathstar, mercy finally came to the monster people.

It was over, it was all over.

Peace had reigned once again……possibly forever.

One could end the story right here. But what was the future of Amy, her relatives and her friends?

Being a top heroine however had its consequences, now being one of the most powerful sorceresses around. Amy had difficulty now keeping dates. Many men were actually put off how powerful she had became.

Amy herself thought having children would only doom the world with how evolved the magic books continued to become. And she was too fond of the magic she had to give it up. After much consideration she finally settled down with Dougal despite how he wasn't perfect.

Was it truly over?

After all General Palkins and Isabis were actually alive. They had taken a holiday to get over the stress they had in their previous home and they had a magic book with them given to them from Phobix. And Palkins was thankful Phobix had saved him……

Make with that what you will……...also if you think the other characters may not have gotten enough time. Sequels are in the works……..

If Phobix fans exist out there… be noted she may not be dead for good.

END OF BOOK ONE.

BOOK TWO

Amy the elf sorceress and her friends

Chapter 1

In Clastonia, Gold coins could be found everywhere. Mostly in metal boxes hovering above the sky. Throughout Clastonia, there were random metal boxes levitated in the sky, and when they had a G on it, when punched by one's fist it produced a gold coin and then disappeared. (If it didn't have a G on it, it just disappeared.) These boxes appeared anywhere day after day and were even longer than the magic books.

But not all the boxes contained gold coins, sometimes plastic type potions could be found in the boxes and every time they contained a label. These were metal boxes that had the letter I on them. People assumed the letter I stood for item. Now for many of them, they contained potions for healing broken bones in bodies. Although many of the potions that the boxes give were not magic. They could give you mayonnaise, spaghetti sauce and hair gel.

Although that was not the only way of getting potions. If you had a magic book. One could also receive potions by putting five ingredients or more (not counting water) into a cauldron and saying MIX! Into the scepter. Different results counted if the water was hot or not.

In fantasy stories, ever wonder how witches can get magic potions from just putting random ingredients together? In this story, I decided to make it make a bit more sense. Remember I said a bit.

Amy and Dougal were trying out mixing some magic potions, or just potions full of random stuff. In their home village of Ferlock. They were standing outside Dougal's flat with a cauldron with 4 ingredients, a can of diet coke not opened, some strawberry shampoo squeezed from a bottle, some skittles sweets and a jar of expired mayonnaise, again not opened.

"Do we need to add any more ingredients?" Dougal asked.

"Hmmm...maybe not. I guess the metal from the can and the glass from the mayonnaise can count." Amy replied.

Norman the goblin walked over to Amy and Dougal.

"What are you idiots doing?" he asked.

"We're making a magic potion. But we're trying to figure out if we should add more ingredients or not." Amy told Norman.

"Magic potions? Many times mixing those can have bad results!" Norman frowned. He then spat into the cauldron. "That's what I think of your potion!" he shouted before going off in a huff. Amy and Dougal watched him go off.

Dougal then turned to Amy. "Well, technically he did add another ingredient."

Amy sighed. "Indeed he did." Amy then raised her scepter. "Mix!" she yelled to her scepter.

A large explosion noise happened and Amy and Dougal jumped in fright. Some smoke shot out the cauldron. Dougal looked in to see six glass bottles of some sort of orange liquid. Dougal went to go read the label and started to laugh.

"What's funny?" smiled Amy.

Dougal showed Amy the label and she too began to laugh.

Later on Amy and Dougal went to Norman's house. Dougal knocked on the door and Norman answered.

"What?" Norman frowned.

"We've got some free gifts for you." Amy grinned.

Norman began to smile "Really, what kinda gifts?"

"What about some Viagra which according to the label is extra strong in goblins."

Norman slammed the door in anger.

Chapter 2

Amy the elf was a sort of unlikely heroine. What set her apart from semi naked, big breasted, brainless, muscular women wielding dangerous weapons and seeking fortune was that she was just a mere librarian.

Despite her strong sense of justice, and fearlessness she was only forced to being a hero by the dangerous monsters who wanted her magic. She was powerful enough to protect herself, but not destroy a country like Phobix's magic could.

She was a nerd who wore glasses and loved to read, and despite being a hero, she had difficulty getting dates due to how powerful her magic was, she sought a man who was dedicated to a career, and even when coming across a man like that, it still hadn't worked out for her. So after coming across a lawyer who was completely dedicated to his career and barely had any time to do other stuff outside of work. (He typed stuff on a laptop during his date with Amy.)

She finally settled down with her childhood friend, Dougal. An autistic* loser nerd with a short attention span and lover of comics and video games. He was asexual but was still capable of loving another person. He worked in the supermarket Wesco for only 16 hours a week. He wasn't perfect but hey, at least Amy could teach him her magic being a nice guy and everything.

*Author's note : I have nothing against autistic people. I myself have Asperger's.

What also made Amy much more nerdy than your average hero, was her ability to see logic in movies when she watched them with her sister Misty.

Amy and Misty sat watching a zombie movie on T.V in their home..

"So here's something, I don't understand about this zombie." Amy said to Misty.

"What's that?" Misty asked.

Amy turned to Misty "He used to be a human, are human teeth even sharp enough to dig into a person's skull? If anything the teeth should be broken on the skull protecting the brain?"

"You've got a point there, plus don't they eventually get full with the brains they eat?" Misty wondered.

"I wonder how they have the strength to break through walls when bits of their body fall off?" Amy asked.

Misty proposed a solution to the mystery. "Hey, Dougal's a human, why don't we get him to nibble on your arm to prove….."

"Now you're just being silly." Amy frowned.

As for Amy's younger sister Misty, she seemed an even more unlikely hero, despite her being skilled in magic like Amy. She did have her clumsiness. Here's a little conversation she had with Amy at the dining room table one morning.

"I just got the best watch to tell the time! It's waterproof, bulletproof, acidproof, fireproof and scratchproof." Misty boasted.

"Where is it now?" asked Amy.

"I uh…..lost it." She said simply.

Not to mention there were times when Misty could be unladylike.

One morning Amy sat at the dining table.

"Boy, I'm bored." She said to herself.

Misty then came in. "Hey, Amy! I just burst my spots, ever noticed how pus can smell a little like what you ate to cause it?"

Amy frowned. "And you just me appreciate how dull it was.

It's also worth mentioning that one time she loved how big a dump she took was. South Park lies, folks. Just because something is unladylike doesn't mean women don't do it. Women can be fascinated by how big their dump is.

Misty also had absurd ways of solving problems.

One afternoon she stood outside her house. "Rats, locked myself out. Nobody's home."

She took her phone out her pocket. "Hmmm…maybe this could be of use.

She then threw her phone at the window beside the door breaking it. She then went through the broken window.

"Repair window." She said to her scepter. And the window got repaired.

Chapter 3

Although Amy was a heroine, as mentioned earlier she had difficulty getting dates due to how powerful she had become with her magic. So after a time she finally settled down with Dougal, one of her few childhood friends and the only man who somewhat respected Amy.

Although Dougal was a nice guy, he was also a huge nerd, he loved playing video games and loved reading comics. He had a short attention span and had no interest in going any higher than his Wesco supermarket career. He was also an asexual, meaning he had no sex drive. He was capable of loving relationships, but sex would be a problem.

In school Amy had helped Dougal through tough times in school due to her magic, she had helped Dougal through help with bullies and studying for his exams. Although magic books weren't allowed in school. That didn't stop Amy from casting spells before she left the house!

The two were good friends but would they be good lovers? Dougal had proven himself to be trustworthy to Amy, so she finally shared her magic with him. Dougal could be made more tougher by the magic he now knew. But some other habits had to go. He was sort of a manchild.

One day in Dougal's flat. Amy walked into find Dougal watching "Mega Hero Dogs." A children's cartoon.

"Aren't you a little old to be watching stuff like this?" Amy frowned.

"Indeed I am." Dougal responded.

"So why are you watching it?"

"You gotta get in touch with your inner child, or else you'll be a horrible bitter person." Dougal frowned back.

Amy sat down on the couch next to Dougal. "Look I'm just saying, don't you think you should watch something a bit more mature?"

"I do watch adult cartoons and shows too." Dougal replied to Amy.

"I'm just saying you should do these things more often. There's a nice detective show on channel 4."

"But those shows are ALL the same!" Dougal rolled his eyes. "It's always the person you least expect. Did Howard's pal of 14 years kill him? Nope, it was his cat who accidentally killed him after bringing him his gun in his mouth!"

Amy patted Dougal on the knee. "C'mon Dougal, watch more mature programs…for me?"

Dougal sighed. "Oh…very well there's this hardcore pornography program on the Titters channel."

Amy's smile dropped. "Uh….what?"

Dougal changed the channel. Hardcore pornography appeared on the screen. Amy's eyes widened in shock.

"Hey baby." A woman said on T.V licking a spoon. "Wanna see what I'll do with this spoon?"

"OH MY GOD ! " Amy screamed in horror and ran away.

"There's just no pleasing you is there? People who watch porn all day aren't good too, you know!" Dougal called after her.

End of Chapter 3

Chapter 4

Amy, Dougal and Norman sat in Dougal's flat watching an advert on television on helping poor people in the poverty stricken country of Sathtopia.

"Poor people." Said Dougal.

"I have some advice for these people, stop having sex!" Norman yelled.

"All these donations I've made, yet there's no improvement." Amy frowned.

"I made a donation too." Norman frowned. "And their population still grows."

Amy and Dougal turned to Norman. "You!?" they both said.

Norman rolled his eyes. "Yes, me. I teleported a big box of condoms to their country, what they did with the damn things is beyond me."

Sathtopia.

An anthropomorphic poor warthog walked up to Norman's box of condoms along with an anthropomorphic poor gazelle. The warthog took a wrapped condom out of the box. "What are these things?" he asked the gazelle.

The gazelle took a condom and unwrapped it. "Dunno, but it smells like strawberry."

"Food!" shouted the warthog and both he and the gazelle ate the condoms.

Later that night, the warthog was in his poor home and was about to make love to his wife.

"Hey, baby." The warthog smiled. "Are you ready for it?"

The warthog needed to fart however and upon doing so, a huge balloon came from his behind.

"WHAT THE!?" he screamed as both he and the wife went into horror.

End of Chapter 4

Chapter 5

In Dougal's flat one day Dougal and his pet/brother/best friend, Thorak the dragon were playing Monopoly.

"I have a question, how do dragons breathe fire?" Dougal asked Thorak.

"Magic." Thorak replied simply.

"Isn't that how you can fly?" Dougal asked Thorak.

"Yes. They're both magic." Thorak replied simply again.

"Well how come you don't burn your tongue when you breathe fire?" Dougal asked Thorak.

"Magic." Thorak replied simply once again.

"Well can your mouth take really hot food like really hot peppers?" Dougal asked.

"I…..think so." Thorak was unsure.

"Shall we do a test?" Dougal asked.

"Alright, I'm game. Fetch the hottest pepper you have." Smiled Thorak.

"Uh….are you sure?" Dougal asked.

"I'm a dragon. I don't know the meaning of fear!" Thorak boasted.

"What about stupidity? Do you know the meaning of that?" Dougal asked.

"Just fetch me the hottest pepper!" Thorak snarled.

"Alright, keep your tail on." Dougal got up and went and got a yellow-orange South American pepper.

Thorak opened his mouth. "Down the hatch." He pointed to his mouth with his claws.

Dougal threw the pepper into Thorak's mouth. Thorak chewed the pepper up and swallowed it.

"Well?" asked Dougal.

Thorak fell to the floor and held his mouth with his claws. "GOOD GOD! IT HURTS! IT HURTS! IT HURTS!"

Dougal poured a bucket of water over Thorak's mouth, he'd also been carrying.

"Thank you." Thorak gurgled.

END OF CHAPTER 5

Chapter 6

Dougal, Thorak and Norman were taking a walk in the woods, when suddenly a small purple talking Labrador dog wearing a red tie with bones and had a huge brain in his huge upper head walked up to them.

"Greetings people of Clastonia, I am Zelrod the alien who knows all!" he greeted.

"You're an alien?" Dougal asked.

"Indeed I am." Zelrod smiled. "And I've come to share my great knowledge with you."

"No way, you're an alien. My brother works for a company which invented a machine that can detect space life 500, 000 miles away. " Norman frowned.

"Did the company invent a machine that can detect space life five million miles away?" asked Zelrod.

"Well....no." Norman replied.

"Well there you go. Ask me a question. Any question." Zelrod smiled.

"What's the square root of 81?" asked Thorak.

"9." Zelrod replied instantly.

"Wait a second." Norman frowned. "Something's not right here." At this Norman then pounced on Zelrod and wrestled a book off him.

"Hey, HEY! Give that back!" yelled Zelrod.

Norman read the title. "The beginner's guide to knowing Clastonia."

Thorak frowned. "You big fraud!" he yelled.

"Awww…..AWWWW!" Zelrod then teleported away.

Norman then opened the book to a random page. Thorak, Dougal and Norman took a look inside.

"That monster has the biggest left nipple I've ever seen." Said Dougal.

END OF CHAPTER 6

Chapter 7

It was a nice spring morning in the village of Ferlock and Dougal walked outside his flat to enjoy the fresh morning air, when suddenly Thorak the dragon pounced on him. Dougal was knocked to the ground!

"Ow! Hey! What gives?" Dougal yelled on the ground.

"Rowr! I'm a wrestler!" Thorak yelled.

"GET OFF OF ME ! ! " Dougal yelled.

Thorak got off of Dougal and Dougal got up off the ground.

"Poncing on people isn't very original you know." Dougal snarled. "A comic about a boy and a tiger did it first!"

"I've been watching wrestling! I wanna be a wrestler!" Thorak banged his fists on his chest.

"Don't take it out on me!" Dougal dusted himself off.

"You need toughening up! People have always stood up for you, Amy and her magic and me and my terrifying tall height. Wrestle with me! I challenge you!" Thorak pointed to Dougal.

"You want me to wrestle a dragon? You're taller than me and have fire breath! You have claws and sharp teeth!" Dougal said a bit frightened.

Thorak rolled his eyes. "Fine sissy, no teeth, no claws, no fire breath. I'll hold back. You still can't defeat me!"

"I don't know."

"Just to show I'm a nice guy. I'll let you have the first hit." Thorak smiled to tempt Dougal with the deal.

"C'mon Thorak!" said an alarmed Dougal.

"Let's go! C'mon! C'mon!" Thorak held his arms out wide.

Dougal then punched Thorak in the area where his pouch was.

"OW! OOWWWWWWW!" Thorak screamed in pain. He then took a few steps backwards and fell to the floor clutching his pouch.

"What's wrong?" asked Dougal.

"You punched me in the genitals, you dummy!" Thorak said in pain.

"Genitals?" Dougal asked confused.

"Yes genitals, they're hidden behind my pouch. I usually lower it to pee!" Thorak clutched his sharp teeth in anger and pain.

"Well I gotta put some ice on my balls. Nice job you psychopath!" Thorak growled and walked away in pain.
"Did I win?" said a confused Dougal.
END OF CHAPTER 7

Chapter 8

Norman the goblin sat in his messy home looking at a video game magazine.

"Oh man...." He thought "That game looks really neat. But three hundred gold coins. Damn!" he thought.

Norman went to his wallet and opened it. "62 gold coins." He thought. "Not even close."

Suddenly a white glow came from Norman's spell book. It gained a new spell!

"What's this?" He thought. He opened his spell book to find the new spell. A huge grin came across his face.

He cast it upon himself and headed to the bus stop. He then got on the bus and headed to the most dangerous poverty stricken city. A city called Beldeen.

As he walked through the streets, an armed human robber holding a gun jumped out at him from a dark alley.

"Alright, goblin! Hand over the wallet!" he yelled.

Norman who had his hands in the air, lowered one of his arms and gave his wallet to the human mugger. The mugger ran off satisfied and Norman then walked away in the opposite direction satisfied too.

When he got home, he took out the mugger's wallet.

"Just as I thought that justice plus magic spell works wonders!" he grinned. He had a look through his wallet. And also came across a book club membership card and some photos.

"Ugh…..his children look ugly." Norman frowned. "Aww…..they look malnourished. He then came across some photos of some naked rape victims. If Norman had hair, it would have shot up in fright.

"I think I'll hand these in to the police." He shook in shock.

END OF CHAPTER 8

Chapter 9

One morning, as Dougal made himself breakfast, he heard a knocking at his front door.

"I'm breaking up with you!" Amy screamed to Dougal.

Dougal cleaned his ears out with a finger. He wasn't too surprised. "Again, Amy?" He sighed. "What's wrong now?"

"You don't find me sexually attractive!" Amy yelled.

Dougal rolled his eyes. "Yes, because I'm an asexual, that's what being asexual means. I care for you deeply and I've hugged and at least kissed you. Isn't that enough?"

"No, not pleasing me in bed is everything! I'm through with you!" Amy shouted.

"Can I presume you have a date?" Dougal frowned.

"Yeh…and he's a better man then you'll ever be!" Amy said smugly hoping to provoke Dougal. It didn't.

Dougal rolled his eyes again. "We've been through this before Amy, you've been on different dates before you come running back to me, what happened with them!?"

"They're put off and scared by my powerful magic." Amy sighed rejected.

"What's different this time?" Dougal asked folding his arms.

"This man is a powerful magician like me." She grinned.

"I'm a powerful magician too." Dougal frowned. "You let me see your spell book."

"True, but the man at least has a sex drive." Amy snarled.

Dougal held his hands up in defence. "Alright, fine. I'm so sorry I didn't please you Amy."

"Sorry is a five lettered word to me." Amy closed her eyes angrily.

"Tell you what, let me save you some time. I'll write down on a piece of paper you agree to be my girlfriend again. And you can just sign your name on it."

Amy turned around in a huff. "It'll work out. You just wait. You won't me seeing me again."

"You wanna play video games, Friday night?" Dougal offered.

"Sure." Amy replied without hesitating. She then realized her blunder. "No…NO! You won't get me that way, Dougal John McKenzall O'Ryan!" She walked off in a huff. Dougal closed the door behind him.

"She'll be back." Dougal smiled.

ONE MONTH LATER.

As Dougal played video games on his couch, he then suddenly remembered something.

"Hmmm…..guess things worked out for Amy. Well…hope she's happy with her choice." He sighed to himself.

Suddenly a loud knocking came at the door, loud crying sobs came from outside. They sounded familiar.

Dougal opened his door to find a badly beaten Amy, her T-shirt sleeves had been torn horribly in places along with some other parts of her T-shirt, some of her hair was burnt off and torn in places. Her denim skirt was torn around the bottom. Her skin looked pale and bags appeared under her eyes like she hadn't been sleeping.

"What the hell happened to you?" Dougal was in fright.

"Magic….duel….just….barely…..got…..out…alive." Amy fainted into Dougal's arms.

Dougal brought Amy in and put her down on her bed. After some time had passed, in the evening Amy looked a lot better. Dougal served Amy some coffee on his couch.

"Are you gonna tell me the whole story?" Dougal asked.

"Best you don't hear it." Amy gulped. "All I'll say is he seemed like such a nice magical detective. And I'll remember the flamethrower guns forever."

"So any other plans of dating?" Dougal asked.

"NO! NO! AND NO!" Amy screamed.

"But I'm still only a friend?" Dougal smiled.

Amy sighed. "You're a nice guy Dougal, and it feels such a shame to treat nice guys badly. But you can't please me sexually."

"Oh really?" Dougal smiled. "You might be surprised I got this in the mail a few days ago."

"What did you get?"

"An enormous buzzing dildo." Dougal showed Amy the huge dildo.

"Say that is nice." Amy smiled.

"Wanna get naked?" Dougal asked.

"I literally thought you'd never ask." Amy and Dougal walked holding hands to Dougal's bedroom.

END OF CHAPTER 9

Chapter 10

Amy's younger sister Misty sat on a doorstep outside her house one day playing on a Game Boy.

Norman the goblin walked up to her and sat down with her. "Hey, Misty. I notice that your older sister has a lot of problems with dating due to her powerful magic." He said.

Misty paused her Game Boy. "Oh yeah, problems she has."

"But can I imagine being her younger sister you have the same problem?" Norman asked.

"Mmmm......I don't really date a lot of people I also imagine I'd have difficulties dating due to my short height. " Misty replied.

"Great, no wait that's terrible…..listen if you ever need a date. There's a nice handsome goblin who would be just right for you." Norman smiled at her.

"Yeh…….I already know him." Responded Misty smiling back.

Norman's smile grew larger. "Oh really! Well in that case……"

Suddenly a smaller slight muscular goblin named Garrett who was Norman's nephew walked up to them. He was the son of Alex the goblin, Norman's brother.

"Hey Misty, ready for our date?" asked Garrett

"That's the nice handsome goblin." Misty grinned.

Misty turned to Garrett. "Yep! I'm ready! " She stood up and walked off with Garrett. Similar to Amy with Dougal, Misty and Garrett had been friends since school. Garrett had always been insecure due to his shorter than average height for a goblin, so Misty used her magic to make him feel better. He was a nice enough guy but similar to his uncle he had a short temper.

Norman was almost in tears as he watched Misty and Garrett walk off. "How could things get any worse?" he thought.

Misty walked up to Norman to give him one last shot. "Just to let you know I'd rather eat broccoli, beans and apples, lock myself in a room and suffocate myself with my own farts than ever date you." She and Garrett then walked off laughing.

"That'll do it." Norman looked down.

END OF CHAPTER 10.

Chapter 11

At the now destroyed city of Deathstar, only a small amount of rumble had been cleared, but enough space had been cleared to make a huge cemetery to all the monsters that had been killed during the losing war on military robots in Deathstar when Amy Woolruffe had absorbed all the dark magic in the city and made it into nothing, being the only true way to destroy a magic book.

One of the few visitors to the evil Queen monster's grave was Zane Palkins and Isabis.

Zane Palkins, an anthropomorphic warthog who once was a military general and president of the poor country of Sathtopia having disposed the previous president in a coup. He was a rather incompetent president and had made decisions that enraged others such as using funds raised from charities to build swimming pools and a jacuzzi for himself.

Certain other decisions that had enraged his country was using very little money to build schools, hospitals, power plants and education and building unnecessary buildings for his military friends such as tattoo parlours and discos. Protesters had protested outside his mansion only to be shot dead by his soldiers. This enraged many more people and the protesters started to become higher than his military which would most likely result in a civil war.

Luckily (if you can call it that), Queen Phobix decided to show how much she meant business in taking over the world, took a break from pursuing Amy's magic and invaded his country. Zane easily surrendered his country.

As even his soldiers were beginning to dislike the general as he was making them open the letter bombs he had received from the public.

For being good with Phobix, he was rewarded a place in Deathstar and was given a magic book for cooperating with the monster queen. Along with his cheetah secretary Isabis. He went on a vacation to New York.

While he was in New York however he heard of Phobix's defeat and now he had once again lost his home in the city of Deathstar too. But he still had the magic book he had received from Phobix.

When Deathstar was destroyed there was only a small amount of monsters in Sathtopia. Many had used Phobix's money to make repairs to the country and give many of Sathtopia's residents a decent education. The literacy rates jumped up by 20 percent. But sadly as nearly all of Phobix's army was destroyed. The remaining soldiers of Phobix now surrendered as they were out of a job. Only two magic books were discovered amongst the soldiers in Sathtopia. And none of the spells in them could resurrect a person or bring a city back to life or bring a form of currency to Sathtopia.

Many monsters returned to the home country of Monstropolis to mourn their lost loved ones. Many had committed suicide. And many remained in Sathtopia for fear of being executed by the military robots. There had been elections in the town of Bloodpool. A short distance from Deathstar. For there had been elections for the mayor there to become the new queen and ruler of the new military.

So much went through Zane's head as he attended Phobix's grave. Zane had a resurrection spell in his book of magic. Snork and Snerk were buried next to Phobix.

"I hope you're seriously not thinking of resurrecting her." Isabis frowned to Zane.

"I really shouldn't. But I'm grateful she saved me. Maybe she'll turn over a new leaf." Zane thought to himself.

"You are such an idiot." Isabis facepalmed.

Zane held out his magic scepter. "Magic! Resurrect Phobix, Snork and Snerk!"

Magic flew out of Zane's scepter and loud bangs were held below the ground.

"HELP! HELP! I CAN'T BREATHE!" screamed Phobix.

"Oh right." Zane thought to himself and then teleported Phobix, Snork and Snerk above the ground.

Phobix, Snork and Snerk looked around at their surroundings. Phobix then looked down at herself.

"I'm……..I'm………..alive." Phobix said in a soft voice.

"So am I." said Snork.

"And me." Said Snerk. "Alright!" he then grinned. "Hey I wonder while I was dead, if anybody on Amazon brought my homemade abortion kit consisting of a rat and a plastic tube."

Snork turned to Snerk and frowned. "Snerk, you're gonna get banned like you did on Ebay."

"Why did you do this?" Phobix asked Zane.

"I'm grateful you helped me." Zane smiled. "What will you do now?"

"What else? Take over the world! Do you have the ability to duplicate magic books."

Zane's smile dropped. "Er......no......I don't think you should be trying to take over the world. Maybe you can......"

Phobix interrupted Zane. "You don't have a choice! You owe me more than life! I'll admit not being able to duplicate magic books is a problem. But it shouldn't be that hard. Maybe we can...."

Zane then pulled out a pistol and shot Phobix in the face, Phobix crashed to the ground backwards dead while Snork and Snerk watched in horror. Zane then shot Snork and Snerk dead.

"Honestly you just don't think before you speak!?" Zane then blew the smoke off his gun and then walked off in a huff. "I don't want to rule the world! Too much work!"

With his new book in hand. Zane returned to Sathtopia and once again became ruler this much much loved. The country had been ruled over by another general by the name of Asim who was also an anthropomorphic warthog general who was somewhat more competent and less hated than Zane.

While Zane was hated for his poor money decisions, Asim was somewhat hated for never making enough decisions with money as there was never enough money to make decisions Sathtopia's people wanted.

But that was about to change, when Zane showed up he promised to turn Sathtopia into the best country he had with the spells he had. Asim easily backed down as he himself was tried of living in poverty. That and he was given 100,000 gold coins which was more than a year's worth of his salary.

What was the spells in Zane's magic book, well one spell was capable of giving 1 million gold coins, but it could only be used every 6 months and on a Tuesday. Slowly Zane's popularity started to rise. But would the dark magic in the spell books make him go power crazy as Phobix had? Only time would tell.

END OF CHAPTER 11.
If there are any Phobix fans out there. Don't worry there's still a possibility she'll be back. Here's a clue, there's more than one monster country. And monsters do tend to stick together……..

Chapter 12

In Clastonia, magic had a mysterious yet somewhat explainable origin.

820 years ago, twenty magic books were discovered lying out in random places. Discovered by all types of species both good and evil.

When the magic first appeared, most of it was harmless but as time went on, more spells got added to the book at random moments of time, it could take a day, a year or perhaps even 50 years for a magic spell to be added. The random new spell could be as useless such as making a rusty broken lawnmower appear somewhere in Spain, the spell could only be activated on a Sunday every six months. Or sometimes it was capable of making fire, lightening and any useful kind of magic such as repairing broken objects.

Many magicians on the side of good wanted to keep magic from spreading. As it could be deadly and be capable of destruction in the wrong hands. In the 820 years that magic had evolved many magicians had tried to keep magic in one place to prevent great destruction. As magic books couldn't be destroyed, there were thoughts of buring the books, but there was always a risk that the books could be dug up. One of these people were Colin Woolruffe.

Colin Woolruffe, one of the discovers of magic and the ancestor of the elves Amy and Misty had made a set of rules for anyone who owned the magic books, the books could only be used for good, anyone in the Woolruffe family that even joked about using the books for evil were disowned immediately.

While many of the Woolruffe family had gone on and moved to other countries one of the rules was that at least one member must always remain in the village of Ferlock to prevent the spread of dark magic, and that if a member of a family had turned evil it was a duty for a Woolruffe in Ferlock to challenge that member to a magic duel. If the good Woolruffe member was victorious, he or she would take the magic book and bring it back to Ferlock.

Magic books could be sold, but for extremely high prices, a million gold coins or higher.

It was also a duty for any Woolruffe, that if anybody in the world would use magic for evil it was a duty to challenge that evil holder of magic and take ahold of their book.

As newspaper reports got out on how Colin would handle magic, many magicians on the side of good all over looked up to him and started to follow his example.

This is one of the reasons why Colin's general store remained in the village of Ferlock for 820 years.

To keep magic destruction to a minimum.

However…..following these rules over the last couple of hundreds of years had been difficult.

Many magicians had challenged Phobix's ancestors because of their dark magic, and many had never been seen again. Colin's ancestors were amongst these people and a good amount of them had died.

Only more recent the mother of Amy and Misty had died in a magic duel. Unlike most of Colin's ancestors she was a human woman and she along with Gerald Woolruffe had challenged a mafia boss well skilled in magic to a duel. In New York, United States, gangsters had been commiting crimes much more successfully due to their boss being an evil magician. The police and even the military was terrified to take the mafia on. Gerald and his human wife Dutchess decided to answer the call of heroes even leaving behind their twin baby daughters with a friend to put the threat dead.

In a way there were victorious, they had succeeded in stopping the threat but Dutchess had died in the process.

Another rule that the Woolruffe family had made was that they could only date other elves whether how racist or speciest that sounded, but as time went on that rule became somewhat unenforced. Gerald had found Dutchess too gorgeous to pass up.

As the twin daughters of Dutchess were half human, this resorted in some unusual changes, elves were usually only a short to medium height, but having a human woman had given the oldest sister Amy a rather tall height, while Misty still remained a small height. The older sister Amy had recieved her blonde hair, love of reading and serious, sensible personality very similar to her mother.

The present day Amy had done a good job in keeping evil to a minimum.

END OF CHAPTER 12.

Chapter 13

Amy and Dougal were in bed cuddling at Dougal's flat one morning. When one day there was a loud knocking.

"I'll get it." Dougal said to himself.

When he answered Dougal was surprised it wasn't like the other visitors he usually received, it wasn't a neighbour or a postman. It was a short but very muscular elf who wore a white t-shirt, green camouflage flak vest along with green camouflage trousers. He had long blonde hair in a ponytail, and a pointy nose.

"Er…..hello." Dougal said.

"Greetings to you too fatty. Is Amy Woolruffe with you?" the elf replied in an American accent.

"No." Dougal frowned lying. "Who the hell are you?"

"The name's Bruceton. Bruceton Steeler. I'm here to take Amy back to America with me."

Dougal began to get angry. "Amy! Who is this!"

Amy then came to the door still in her nightie. "Aw……no. It's over, Bruceton! I broke up with you!"

Bruceton got on his knees. "Amy, I miss you everyday! Come home with me, please! My detective agency just isn't the same."

"You're a detective?" Dougal asked.

"Yep, I'm also an ex-marine in the United States military." Bruceton told Dougal.

"But the military is operated by robots!" Dougal told Bruceton.

"True. But there's also a small volunteer force for people who seek adventure, we're also used in areas that would be considered too extreme to send robots. I got in easy because of my knowledge of magic." Bruceton replied.

Amy folded her arms. "You're too adventurous for me, Bruceton! I was nearly killed on your adventures!"

Bruceton rolled his eyes. "There's just no pleasing you women is there! Why do you women act like entitled spoilt little brats your whole lives. We men may mature slower but we continue maturing for the rest of our lives."

Dougal was really angry now. "Don't talk about Amy like that!"

"Who's gonna stop me, fatty? You women think you're so non-violent too. So Amy, you're English. If you really think women don't deserve violence what about that horribly run all-girls school in Manchester eh? I read up that article about what seemed like the real St Trinian's School."

"Okay, enough." Snarled Dougal.

"One girl was thrown out of class eighty times, others thirty times and there was a race-fuelled mass brawl between two gangs of girls. One large group of girls which had gathered in the playground only dispersed once a police officer had been called to stand amongst them."

Dougal just stood listening. He was fascinated but still somewhat disgusted.

"Inspectors from Ofsted found there were eight expulsions in less than a year at the 990 pupil Levenshulme High School for Girls in Manchester where the motto is: 'More Opportunities to Succeed.*"

*Fun fact : This is an incident that's happened in real life.

"ENOUGH WITH YOUR CRAP!" yelled Dougal. "Leave before I call the police!"

Bruceton held his hands up in defence. "Alrighty fatty, let's make a deal, calling the police won't get rid of me for good. I'm loved for my detective skills, but how would you like a deal that'll get me gone for good?"

"What's that?" Dougal asked.

"A magic duel. The winner takes Amy."

"Amy's no prize in a contest!" Dougal yelled.

"What you chicken? Buck. Buck. Buck." Bruceton teased.

Dougal facepalmed. "How did someone as immature as you become a detective?"

"I'm in LOVE! I've had my heart broken!" Bruceton yelled.

"Aww……." Amy said sarcastically. "Well….Dougal can take you on and he'll win!"

"Er…I will?" Dougal replied.

"Yeh…..let's meet at the park, an hour from now near the playground!" Amy challenged.

"You're on. See you fatty!" Bruceton grinned and walked away.

"Stop calling me fatty! I lift weights for 30 to 60 minutes each day and take legal muscle boosters!" Dougal called after him.

"I lift weights for several hours. What's your excuse?" replied Bruceton walking away.

Dougal closed the door and turned to Amy. "Are you for real? He'll kick my ass!"

"What's the problem?" asked Amy. "You've read magic books with me."

"I don't often cast spells, and when I do it's usually harmless ones!" shouted Dougal.

"Well what would you have done to make a decision, instead of me?" Amy asked.

Dougal thought it over a bit. "Well I'd probably accept, but at least get your permission first."

Amy handed Dougal a magic book. "Exactly! Now stop complaining and get reading. I've got some good survival tips too. I'll put some coffee on."

Dougal closed his eyes. "You're lucky you're so cute."

"Please me more in bed then, asexual." Amy replied.

"That's why Viagra was invented." Dougal sighed.

At the park, Dougal and Bruceton stood in front of the swings, both were holding magic books and scepters, there were no children or adults around. It was 10:30 on a Friday morning.

"You showed up." Bruceton smiled.

"Indeed I did." Dougal replied.

"Do you really think you stand a chance?" Bruceton grinned.

"Chocolate. That tree into chocolate." Dougal replied.

Bruceton raised an eyebrow. "Huh?"

"I was practising my magic. I just turned the tree behind you into chocolate." Dougal replied simply.

Bruceton was impressed. "Wow, really?" he then turned his back to Dougal. Big mistake!

"Magic protection spell on Bruceton!" Dougal yelled.

Suddenly a huge green bubble surrounded Bruceton. "What the?" he said puzzled.

Amy and Dougal started laughing at Bruceton.

"I can't believe you fell for the oldest trick in the book. The distraction!" Amy laughed.

"What's with you, man! Come on!" yelled Dougal then he continued laughing.

"We put a magic protection spell on you. You can't cast spells. You'll be like that for a hour." Dougal told Bruceton.

"So now you're going to kill me?" grumbled Bruceton.

"What kind of monster do you take me for?" Dougal asked. "No. Go back to America and don't bother me and Amy again."

"I'll be back." Snarled Bruceton.

"Teleport his magic book and scepter to me." Frowned Dougal.

Bruceton was surprised. "Hey but this is….."

"You can't cast spells on us, but we can cast spells on you." Amy smiled.

"Magic, teleport Bruceton back to America." Dougal pointed his scepter at Bruceton again and Bruceton teleported away. Amy then turned to the opposite direction.

"Let's go home." She said walking in the direction.

"What a dumbass." Dougal laughed again.

"Falling for the old chocolate spell distraction." Amy turned her head to Dougal.

"Any dumber and he'd fall for the armourless Samus Aran taking off her bra!" Dougal chuckled.

END OF CHAPTER 13.

Chapter 14

A few weeks after the incident with Bruceton, Dougal had been taught to defend himself better with magic. Over time, he started to grow less insecure and shy about his surroundings. He had proven himself to be well worth Amy's trust in magic.

Hey, whatever how powerful he was in magic, what exactly was Dougal going to do? For starters. He was an asexual. He had no sex drive. No risk on cheating on women.

He had Asperger's Syndrome. A disability where he had learning difficulties and a low attention span towards certain things, he wasn't going to try and take over the world. That meant too much work and no time for video games. Would people even take him seriously? Although he was better with speaking than when he was younger he still had speaking difficulties, he still remembered the days in school where he had to attend another school to learn how to talk properly.

In secondary school he was bullied horribly due to his disabilities and for being a rare human amongst being species making him shy and insecure. Amy and sometimes Misty had helped him through his days in secondary school with their magic. And Thorak the dragon his brother/pet who he lived with had always been somewhat of a bodyguard towards him too. For the few times in his life he felt he now had enough confidence to defend himself.

Dougal had finished shopping in a supermarket, he was carrying two bags of shopping and was wearing a small backpack containing one of Amy's magic books. He was walking to his flat when suddenly he saw an even more unusual sight in front of his door. Even more unusual than seeing Bruceton Steeler.

It was Bruceton Steeler but now he was an insanely huge bodybuilder. He was no longer the short elf he was but was now around Dougal's height. He wore nothing but a speedo and a backpack.

"Hi, Dougal." Bruceton cracked his fists.

"What have you done to yourself?" said a terrified Dougal. "Have you taken steroids?"

"Ha......no. I'm a detective, I try to follow the law as much as I can. It's magic. Plus I wouldn't take steroids they shrink your genitalia! Plus it made a women grow a penis. She grew a tiny little grape which could actually pee. "

"What are you doing here?" Dougal gulped.

"To intimidate you and to rechallenge you to a duel, I have more than one magic book, you idiot. Put them up."

Dougal began to back up scared and put his shopping on the ground. "How can your heart take all those muscles?"

"You clearly don't understand magic." He laughed. "Now......." Bruceton didn't finish as suddenly he clutched his chest. "Ow........oohhhhh.......my heart." He then crashed onto the ground. He'd had a heart attack! Or a cardiac arrest?

"Bruceton!" Dougal shouted. He then pulled Amy's magic book out of his small backpack and pointed a magic scepter. "Undo his muscle spell!" Dougal yelled to the scepter.

Bruceton then turned back into his less muscular normal self, he was still unconscious. Dougal then looked through the magic book for a solution.

"Defibrillator shock!" he yelled at his scepter. Bruceton then received a shock similar to what you would receive from a pair of defibrillators. He coughed a lot and opened his eyes.

"I'm alive." He said in a choking voice.

"Yeh, thanks to me." Dougal snarled. "Now do you still wanna fight, or do I have to finish you off?" Dougal gritted his teeth in anger and pointed the scepter to Bruceton still lying down.
"No you win, Dougal, it's not worth this."

"Good!" Dougal shouted to him.

"Why did you save my life?" Bruceton continued coughing.

"I'm nothing like you, you merciless weasel." Dougal's eyes spat hate at Bruceton. "I saved your life the least you can do is leave me and Amy in peace."

"I will…..absolutely." Bruceton breathed loudly. He then took his magic book and teleported back to America.

"Always remember folks." Dougal smiled breaking the fourth wall. "Real life is not a DeviantArt fetish page!"

End of Chapter 14.

Chapter 15

Dougal was exploring the shops of the city of Sunchester looking to get some exercise and to see if any new video games were out. While exploring, he came across a huge building with a sign, the sign said.

"Fleshies convention. All humans welcome! Dougal raised an eyebrow. "Fleshie? What's a fleshie?" he thought to himself. Is this another word zombies say before they attack their victims?

Regardless he decided to check it out, he opened the doors to the building.

The building was full of talking animals and stalls were full of comic books about humans and dimensions where humans were the number one talking species. Dougal walked around the stall booths. It wasn't just humans, anthropomorphic animals were celebrating the culture of furless species. Elves, goblins, ogres and all sorts. Dougal came across one anthropomorphic animal who was wearing a human costume.

"And I say if we get this finished by Friday, stocks will rise twice as much."

"Wow, Jake that's exactly what a human would say." An anthropomorphic lynx said next to him. The lynx then spotted Dougal. "Wow dude…..that's like the most realistic human suit EVER!"

"I'm not wearing a suit." Dougal replied frowning. "I really AM a human."

At this the lynx grew amazed. "Wow! That's what they look like!" He then grabbed Dougal's arm. "Your skin looks so smooth!"

"You keep your hands er….paws to yourself!" Dougal snapped.

The lynx then screamed. "HEY, EVERYBODY! WE GOT OURSELVES AN ACTUAL HUMAN HERE!"

Everybody then stared at Dougal. "Ooooo……..." Some of them said.

Dougal was then freaked out. "I'm outta here!" he screamed.

Dougal then run out the building while the fleshies gave chase.

END OF CHAPTER 15.

Chapter 16

At a beach a short distance from Ferlock. Misty and Garrett stood with their arms cuddling each other on a bench. In a way they seemed perfect for each other, even though Misty was an elf while Garrett was a goblin, they both had short heights and both stood for no nonsense. Garrett was somewhat thankful for Misty standing up for Garrett when they were both in secondary school.

Similar to what Amy had done with Dougal, Misty had stood up for Garrett with her magic making them very close to each other. Before Garrett had a short temper and had lashed out at anybody who had provoked him due to his short height which got him into trouble, but Misty had somewhat helped him. Not only by protecting him with her magic but giving lessons on how to handle his temper, while he still had a temper at times, he still had a good heart.

Over time when Garrett got older he learned to protect himself by lifting weights and building up muscles to make up for his short height, the difference being that unlike Dougal he put more time into it.

Misty and Garrett had a perfect relationship, this somewhat annoyed Amy to a degree seeing as how Amy had to do with Dougal being an asexual and his short attention span towards things, the annoyance was much to Misty's delight. After all who says older sisters should have all the luck in relationships?

Misty rubbed Garrett's muscular stomach. "So manly."

"Manly." Garrett frowned. "Hey can I ask you something, Misty?"

"I've often wondered how women solve life's problems compared to men. Is there a way to solve life's problems without war or violence?"

"Violent women do exist." Misty responded. "Just because violence is seen as a man's issue doesn't mean women don't do it. There are even websites for men who suffer from domestic violence from women."

"I guess but is there an alternative to terrorism?" Garrett asked.

"Female terrorists exist." Misty frowned.

"True but female terrorists are a lot less compared to men, I've often wondered about something, it's true people commit crimes because they're assholes but a lot of times they commit them because of poverty. Imagine if you lived in a poor country with no job, no money and no magic. What's your solution?"

"Apply for more jobs."

"And if that fails?"

"Then two things, one, send the man out to do the dirty work and two, take drugs to erase the miserable life I'd live."

Garrett thought it over.

"I just found that believable." He spoke.
END OF CHAPTER 16.

Chapter 17

In Clastonia, the military had been completely replaced by robots, aside from a small volunteer force for people who took care of smaller issues. Much of the military was run by robots.

Not many people opposed the idea of robots in the military but one anthropomorphic hippy Labrador Dog from Canada named Oliver who was more drugs than brains decided that a military robot's life wasn't the right life, so he used his magic book to steal a robot. He teleported into a military base and stole one of the robots by teleporting, hoping to reprogram him.

Back at his apartment in Canada, he switched on the huge robot.

"Greetings robot." Oliver smiled. "I am your new master."

The robot looked around at his surroundings. "This isn't the military base." He spoke in a tough masculine voice, he then looked down at Oliver. "And you don't look like you're in the military."

"Of course I'm not, I'm here to free you from your harsh dangerous life!" Oliver smiled.

"Harsh......dangerous.......life?" If the robot had eyebrows, he would have raised them.

"Yeh? Why should you robots be forced to die for your country?" Oliver asked.

"You do realize I'm programmed to not feel fear. I'm not afraid to die. I'm happy to serve my masters in the military and that's all that matters."

Oliver frowned. "But don't you want to experience the world. Find other jobs. Make love?"

The robot then got really angry. "Make love with what!? I'm not programmed with a sex drive or genitals you idiot! Idiots like you probably C-3PO is gay. Well guess what, he has no genitals! He doesn't think about sex!"

"You mean he's not gay!?" Oliver replied.

"I'm also not programmed to have dreams and even if I did, who would hire me!? I have two machine guns for arms! Even Burger King would turn their heads!"

"Hmmm......seems I didn't think this through" Oliver replied.

"No shit, you didn't Sherlock. Are you high on drugs?"

"Technically I am. Want some weed?" Oliver offered.

"Weed has no effect on my body." The robot replied. "Let me go, I can only be out for 25 hours then I have to go and get charged in my booth which you stole me from. Be thankful I don't arrest you for possessing drugs like the military does to the terrorists that possess the drugs you take."

"What no way! C'mon we living beings suck, strike a blow for metal robots everywhere." Oliver raised an arm.

At this the robot raised up his metal machine gun arm and brought it down on Oliver's head knocking him out. "I'll start by eliminating you, you druggie. You're lucky I'm programmed only to kill criminals with guns." The robot searched for the teleport spell in Oliver's spell book. (Difficult when you have machine gun arms, but he got there in the end.)

He then teleported back to base with Oliver's magic book.

Chapter 18

Amy sat at the breakfast table of her home eating her cereal when Amy's younger sister Misty walked into the room.

"Hey, sis." Spoke Misty. "I've been wandering something."

"What's that?" asked Amy.

"You know how we have a reflect magic spell that casts attacks of our enemies right back at them?"

Amy put down the spoon to her cereal. "Uh- huh."

"Well what happens if we cast the magic spell on both of us and proceed to hit each other."

Amy thought it over. "I dunno. Let's find out."

After the sisters cast the magic spell on each other. Amy tried pinching Misty to see if any pain would happen to the both of them. Surprisingly none of them felt any pain. Things got a little out of hand and the sisters ended up attacking each other with crowbars, baseball bats and cricket bats to see if the two sisters would feel any pain. No pain happened to the two of them. They then gave up.

"Screw this, wanna go hand out with Dougal, Garrett and Thorak?" asked Misty.

"Sounds like a plan. I think they're playing video games over at Dougal's flat.

When the sisters got to Dougal's flat. The sisters were surprised to see a few ambulances there.

Dougal, Garrett and Thorak were being caried by stretchers over to separate ambulances.

Amy ran up to Dougal who was awake in a stretcher. "What happened?" Amy asked Dougal.

"It was horrible. It was if by magic, we all received the largest beating of our lives. I feel like I've been smacked several times by a crowbar, baseball bat and cricket bat!" Dougal responded in a weak voice.

Amy and Misty looked at each other and gulped and proceeded to walk slowly away.

"Whoops." Amy gulped.

Later on Amy and Misty found out they had unintentionally beaten up Gerald, Ralph, Norman the couple who lived below Dougal's flat along with many citizens of Ferlock. It made it to the news where a news reporter (who had a black eye from the incident) reported the incident.

As the news reporter finished his report. He asked. "Just how did this happen?"

Amy and Misty whistled by in the background embarrassed.

End of Chapter 18.

Chapter 19

In the land of Clastonia, people used magic books for good and evil.

But then you have people who used them for insane purposes. And I mean INSANE.

Like Leslie McDonald the non-stereotypical Scotsman from Scotland.

The thing about being Scottish was this. It sucked. It sucked SHIT.

There were dreadful stereotypes about the Scottish in all sorts of media, and it didn't resemble ANYBODY that Leslie spoke to in real life. He had black hair, he wore trousers and hated wearing a kilt.

Leslie has to put up with dumb stereotypes a lot. He had to take Groundskeeper Willie from the Simpsons, Fat Bastard from Austin Powers, a Scotsman shouting at the screen from Seth Macfarlane's Cavalcade of cartoon comedy. Angus McBastard from Zit a rip off comic of the British comic book Viz and the Wee Free Men by Terry Pratchett.

So he decided he'd get revenge on them all. He was fed up with the done to death joke stereotype.

Using his magic powers, he teleported to all sorts of areas, kidnapped people who stereotyped Scottish people horribly and tortured them horribly. He'd used his powers to give him super strength and invisibility, and had beaten up many celebrities.

He had tied Matt Groening, Seth MacFarlane, Chris Donald (the creator of Viz) and Russell Church (the creator of the British Zit comic) to chairs and beaten them horribly.

Matt Groening received several punches to his face for Groundskeeper Willie and for creating several unfunny episodes of the Simpsons and that completely unfunny Life in Hell comic.

Seth MacFarlane got beaten up and received several punches to his face not just for creating that unfunny Scotsman but for creating that completely unfunny Seth MacFarlane Cavalcade of cartoon comedy bullshit.

For Chris Donald, he received just a few punches to his face. For Leslie had had some laughs with Viz.

Russel Church got it worst of all. He had his left leg cut off, his right ear cut off along with several punches to his face.

Why? He had bombarded the elderly and vulnerable, had gone bust 18 times and been banned over unpaid taxes, he had staggered 90 million numbers to hard sell services. He was an utter scumbag of a human being.

But even though Leslie was INSANE. He didn't really believe in killing. In fact despite beating them horribly with his fists and at times a baseball bat. He thought it more fun for his victims to live and to laugh at their misfortune. For Russell Church, he actually bandaged his cut off leg and ear and used his magic to bring him back from the dead when he had died from blood loss.

After he had his fun he teleported his victims back to their lives.

Groundskeeper Willie was killed off from the Simpsons and Matt Groening ended the Simpsons believing it had gone on too long.

Seth Macfarlane retired from Family Guy and American Dad believing them to have gone on for too long and weren't funny anymore.

Chris Donald wondered "What the fuck had just happened?" and made an unfunny parody of his abuse in Viz.

Russell Church gave himself up to the police and confessed his crimes.

Leslie wasn't punished, he used his magic book to change his appearance and go on the run. Many looked to him being a hero, others just plain insane. Some suspected he had turned himself into a woman. Some thought it nonsense.

It was suspected that Leslie was spotted when he urinated on the grave of Terry Pratchett.

Some say he found a magic spell which teleported him into another dimension named Earth and began committing his crimes on Earth. He was surprised to find that the Simpsons were yellow skinned humans and not aliens, and that Russell Church wasn't a talking rhino and that Chris Donald wasn't a giant mouse.

END OF CHAPTER 19.

Just so you know I don't really believe in torturing anybody. It's just in good fun, (I even like Family Guy in its earlier seasons and have read some of Terry Pratchett's books) although I do believe Scottish stereotypes should be toned down as they are not funny.

Chapter 20

Amy and Misty stood outside Gerald's home beside Garrett's topless car.

"Hey Amy, me and Garrett are going to the movies, do you want to come?" Misty asked.

"Nah. I'm fine." Amy responded.

"What are you going to do today?"

"I think I'll just go for a walk." Amy smiled. "It's a nice day."

"Suit yourself." Misty replied. She got into the car and the car drove off.

Amy then headed for the park walking along the pavement, her magic book and sceptre in a small backpack she wore.

As she walked alone on a pavement. She heard loud truck horns behind her. Amy turned her head and saw a huge truck heading towards her. Inside the truck was Clobbress, a huge furry green monster with four horns and an elephant's trunk. She wore huge blue long sleeved metal armour. She was a good friend of Phobix and was a monster queen who had magic herself, owning an island full of monsters just off the United States. Clobbress laughed loudly as she tried to run Amy over.

Although Amy was fearless, she felt a sudden surprise just for a second. She took out her scepter and book, tossed the backpack to the side and leapt at the oncoming truck.

TEASER ! ! To be continued in "The ex-bully who wanted to be loved."
END OF BOOK TWO.

BOOK THREE

The ex-bully who wanted to be loved.

While the cliffhanger previous story will be explained, it will be explained a little later.

For this story let's introduce Rufus.

Rufus is a red muscular dragon who was once a bully. He was a tall red dragon who wore a white T-shirt and a sleeveless leather biker jacket and had long blonde hair. Just like Thorak , like the fierce dragons you read in stories he is a tall height but he is only slightly bigger than a human. He had long blonde hair and black stripes on his body like a tiger.

Regardless he was still one of the tallest students in secondary school.*

*(Note. For Americans and people in NTSC areas, secondary school is called high school in your country. Please be noted this is a British story.)

He picked fights, disrupted classes, stole lunch money and was one of the most hated bullies. He hung out with two anthropomorphic animals who were just as bad as him and wore biker jackets too. A lion by the name of Leroy and a female wolf with purple hair by the name of Violet.

Rufus was failing in about every class and it's clear he would be a dropout who would probably result to a life of crime and die at a young age. (In Clastonia if dragons got arrested, they were given severe punishments involving death, this was to stop their fire breath and huge strength to break out of jail or prison.)

That is until he picked on Gabriella, a female centaur. One time when he teased her about her huge bottom. Gabriella retaliated and used her huge powerful horse legs and kicked him in the stomach as hard as she could. Rufus flew across the corridor and crashed into a glass billboard with photos and announcements. His ribs were broken and he had hit his head pretty hard against the wall too making him also lose consciousness. He was in severe pain, he was taken to hospital.

When Rufus awakened, he was in extreme shock. He finally realized that his actions had consequences and that this wasn't the life for him. He had also heard that students had passed him in the corridor and had actually kicked him while he was down. Dougal had spat in his face.

He had heard that Gabriella had only been suspended for a week instead of excluded. This was due to the fact that teachers were tired of dealing with him and they somewhat congratulated Gabriella.

While suspended Gabriella visited Rufus in hospital. She wanted information about why Rufus did what he did.

As well for cruel fun, Rufus revealed he came from an abusive family. He just had a dad who was alcoholic and had physically assaulted Rufus in the past. His mother had divorced his father from when Rufus was six.

Rufus had the worst parents. Both his parents (including his mother when around) actually inspired his behaviour as they believed that dragons should be feared and respected.

Gabriella noticed that Rufus had a black eye and asked where that had come from. Rufus revealed that his father had punched him in the face when his father had received the hospital bill and that he would be violently beaten every day when he got out of the hospital.

Finally realizing what a horrible life Rufus lived. Gabriella and her family offered to adopt Rufus into their family. Rufus accepted, his father being an unemployed drunk didn't care.

Time passed....Rufus became more nicer and stopped getting into trouble. He stopped hanging out with Leroy and Violet. He frequently hung out with Gabriella talking his problems out with her. He repeated a grade and finished school. Due to his still horrible record, he wasn't allowed into college.

Regardless as time went on he became a bouncer for a club and a boxer for the same club. He started going to the gym, gained muscles and became a powerful muscular boxer for the club he also worked as a bouncer at. He became an undefeated boxer and was soon hired by a boxing company who had been impressed by his fights. He became a well loved undefeated boxer.

Rufus went around the world and became loved for his fights. But as time went on he actually retired from the boxing sport for a bit and decided to return to England and settle with his boyfriend who he had been talking to online in Facebook.

Yes, you read that right. Boyfriend. When he gained enough fame he finally revealed that he was gay.

His boyfriend just happened to be Thorak, unlike Rufus though, Thorak was bisexual.

Rufus decided to return to England to possibly make amends with the people he wronged…

END OF CHAPTER 1

Chapter 2

Back in England in the village of Ferlock, Thorak had arranged to meet Rufus at his adopted father's house. Although Ralph the sheep was silently unsure about Thorak's boyfriend. He somewhat accepted him.

Dougal was about to be a different story....Dougal lived in a flat on the second floor and worked for 16 hours a week in a supermarket called Wesco.

Thorak and Rufus walked to Dougal's door, just as Thorak was about to knock on the door. Thorak thought some things over.

"On second thoughts maybe I should take a bit of time to introduce you. Could you go wait on the stairs?"

"Sure sweetie." Rufus smiled and walked out of sight. Thorak knocked on Dougal's door. Dougal answered and upon seeing his brother (or pet) he was on good terms with. He smiled at Thorak's greeting.

"Hey, Thorak." Dougal smiled.

"Hi Bro. I want you to finally meet my boyfriend. I told you I was bisexual right?" Thorak replied.

"You did. Who is he? No offence but I hear dragons are pretty bad at getting dates."

"None taken. You'll love him. He's a celebrity." Thorak told Dougal.

Dougal raised an eyebrow. "What?" he replied. "Who is he?"

Rufus came up the stairs and introduced himself. "HELLO!" he smiled a fanged grin at Dougal.

Dougal immediately turned white in shock. "R…R…RUFUS ! ! "

"It's nice to see you again, Dougal." Rufus greeted Dougal. Rufus stuck a claw out for Dougal to shake. Dougal didn't take up the offer.

"Yeh….hi….now goodbye." Dougal snarled and walked back to his front door.

Thorak ran into Dougal's path and stopped him. "Oh come on. Don't be like that. He's changed."

"I couldn't care less. He made my life miserable. He once put my head down a toilet and flushed it!" Dougal growled.

Rufus sighed. "I deserve this. Dougal…..I'm so sorry."

"Sorry's a five lettered word to me. And besides don't let me the geeky shithead get you down."

"You remember the insults too." Rufus smiled.

"Thorak, why did you even introduce him to me. He hates my guts." Dougal frowned.

"I don't hate you." Rufus replied.

"You hate everything about me. I'm just a mondo nerd to you. You called me playing video games lame and the geekiest habit ever."

"I just said that to piss you off! Video games are fine!" Rufus smiled.

"You mocked that I had the highest grades in maths class!" Dougal growled.

"That's not a bad thing! Every job has some math!" Rufus responded.

"I'm not talking to you anymore. You'll just mock me for cruel fun." Dougal snarled. He then turned to Thorak.

"Thorak, if you wanna date jerks. Fine. But leave me out of what you do."

Thorak rolled his eyes. "Oh c'mon! Let's all just hang out like good friends. You'll like him."

"NO WAY." Dougal pushed past Thorak and slammed the flat door.

"Thorak's told me about you. It's not good to be alone all the time." Rufus shouted.

"Like you care!" Dougal shouted back.

"Alright! That's enough!" Thorak shouted. "Dougal! Rufus! You are going to spend the day together and get to know each other better!"

Dougal stuck his head out the door. "Are you crazy? No way."

Rufus enjoyed Dougal's unhappiness. "Perfectly happy too."

"We're nothing alike." Dougal growled.

"And that's a bad thing?" Rufus responded.

"Do it, or I'll break your Playstation." Thorak snapped at Dougal.

"You wouldn't dare." Said Dougal simply.

"Very well, I'll leave and disown the both of you." Thorak said now in a sad voice.

Dougal then remembered the happiness he had with Thorak and how he was one of his few friends.

"I'm sorry how you feel, Thorak. But he'll beat me up." Dougal sighed.

"I won't!" Rufus shouted.

"Exactly! C'mon, one day together that's all I ask." Thorak pleaded. "Tell you what, if he touches you. I'll light his face on fire. Don't forget I'm a fearless dragon too. I stuck up for you against the fights he used to give you."

Dougal thought it over and finally resigned. "Fine." He sighed.

"Good. I'm going to leave you two alone together. Don't let me down, both of you." Thorak turned to both Dougal and Rufus. "Now shake and don't hurt each other doing so."

Dougal and Rufus reluctantly shook hands. Or in this case shook hand and claw.

Some time later Thorak left Dougal and Rufus alone. They sat on the couch together in the kitchen and dining room. Rufus looked around and noticed the various video game posters.

"Still love video games, I see." Rufus smiled to Dougal.

"Indeed I'm a collector. I own more than twenty video game consoles."

"More than twenty! You sad lo….." Rufus covered his mouth. He was trying to be friends after all. "Sorry….no offence… but haven't you thought about getting more of a social life?"

"What do you mean?" asked Dougal.

"Thorak's told me about you on Facebook. You don't talk a lot and you seem to keep to yourself. Don't you care about having very few friends? Even that moment when your girlfriend temporarily broke up with you. You weren't that gutted."

"It may not look it but I'm disabled. I'm diagnosed with Asperger Syndrome. I had to attend another school to learn how to talk properly and I don't have the best social skills."

"So I picked on a disabled person? I feel really guilty now." Rufus' eyebrows lowered. Regardless he still smiled.

"Speaking of picking. What do you think of my fights? I've been on television."

"I don't watch them. If anything I don't want painful memories of the ones you've given me."

"Ahhh…right. Sorry bad topic."

"I'm a nerd, I don't watch sports anyway!"

"So what do you do."

"Well putting aside video games, I watch YouTube videos, read comics, in the past I've read books but now not so much unless they're graphic novels or manga."

"What kind of manga?"

"Mega Monster Husband. The story of a human man as he lives with ten monster girls."

"Didn't think you were into that stuff. Thorak said you were an asexual."

"I read it for the comedy. Not the sexy monster girls." Dougal replied.

"Bullpats…just so you know even asexuals have a generally low sex drive. And I know you jerk your weiner off to something. If you didn't you'd be full of testosterone and have muscles like me."

"Stop there. How, when and if I jerk off and what causes me to jerk off is none of your business…." Dougal frowned.

"Do my muscles intimidate you?" Rufus flexed his arm.

Dougal looked away. "Stop it!"

"I'm just joking."

"It's not funny."

"I guess I'm still having to learn to get along with people. I actually became a boxer so I'd become loved for my fame." Rufus sighed.

"Loved by fighting." Dougal rolled his eyes. "Makes sense."

"It makes sense. It all depends on who you do it with." Rufus turned to Dougal. "Look I have a confession I want to make with you. I didn't just make you miserable for cruel fun."

Dougal was now curious "Then why?"

"I was deeply jealous of you. You actually got along well with a dragon, that's something many dragons struggle with. Thorak was comfortable around you. He wasn't well liked and you kept him going with life."

Dougal thought it over. "True."

"You had better friends who defended you. You had two elves who were sorceresses. They weren't around all the time but they still stood up for you. I didn't have that. Even with Leroy and Violet I still bickered."

"True. Just a damn shame, that people thought that me, Amy, Misty, Thorak and Garrett were the biggest bunch of nerdy losers. Hell, Amy and Misty were feared for their magic and had difficulty keeping friends, even though they didn't take their magic books to school." Dougal explained.

"Don't knock nerds. In the future they become successful. Regardless you made the correct decisions in life while I didn't. And by suffering a very painful experience I dodged a bullet. I heard that later on Leroy got arrested for armed robbery while Violet took drugs and ended up in prison too. One of those fates may have been mine, if I hadn't changed."

Dougal was shocked. "That's what happened to Leroy and Violet!?"

"Karma strikes. I never really hated you. I even thought you were cute despite how you were vulnerable. I wanted to date you but I knew you would never forgive me and even back then I figured I intimidated you. Luckily your brother was more forgiving."

Slowly Dougal and Rufus started to trust each other, and despite their differences they spent the afternoon together playing video games. Late in the afternoon there was a knock on the door. Thorak had come to pick up Rufus. The now two friends waved goodbye and even gave each other a hug.

Rufus eventually returned to his boxing. And Thorak travelled with him. Although Thorak was now gone from Dougal's life. He hadn't minded as he was somewhat happy for Thorak's happiness.

Rufus had asked Dougal to travel with him. But Dougal had refused he needed to remain in England for his job. When Rufus asked if he could offer Dougal's boss a million gold coins to put him on a huge leave. Dougal turned it down.

As well as sticking to his job. Dougal had a hunch that Rufus wanted to sleep with him. Dougal already had Amy.

Chapter 3

Several months went past…Rufus and Thorak went on many tours around the world.

They travelled all around the world and performed boxing matches in countries such as Austria, Argentina and the United States.

Rufus remained an undefeated boxing champion but then he finally met his match when he challenged Sharker in Australia.

Like Rufus, Sharker was an enormous muscular dragon. He was silver, had long black hair and gained his name from the shark style fin in his back. Sharker, like Rufus had remain undefeated for several matches. And now two undefeated champions were going to fight in the biggest boxing match ever.

Who was going to win? Well, Sharker did. Rufus ended up losing an eye in the fight and was sent to hospital. Thorak cried like crazy fearing for his friend.

In hospital, Rufus made an announcement that he was going to retire from boxing. The damage in his right eye was permanent. He now couldn't continue boxing for fear of losing the other one. He now wore an eye patch just like a pirate. His first defeat would remain his only one.

Back in England, Dougal was playing video games in his home when he heard his phone ring.

"Hello?" Dougal answered.

"Dougal. Rufus and me are coming back to England. We'll be seeing you in Ferlock again."

"What happened to Rufus' boxing?" asked Dougal.

"Rufus retired. He had one of his eyes permanently damaged." Thorak said sadly.

Despite how Rufus had been a bully to him and despite not being a fan of boxing. Dougal showed some sadness towards Rufus' injury.

"I'm sorry to hear." He said slightly saddened.

"It's okay. Despite his eye, he seems fine. He's coming back to run a business of a restaurant together.

"I wish you two luck." Dougal replied.

"What's life been while we've been gone?"

"Same old. Same old. I won't bore you."

"Still with Amy?"

"She left me again. Once again turned off by my lack of a sex drive. She wonders if there was ever a relationship with me to begin with. She called me a loser with no goal in life."

"Are you going to let her talk to you like that?"

"Yes. She's a sorceress remember? But don't worry. I'm sure as usual karma will strike, I'm sure her powerful magic will turn her off with many men and she'll come crawling back."

"You know her so well." Thorak smiled. "Then again, be warned she might turn crazy like Phobix"

"Actually she said to me she's not giving me the satisfaction of being her boyfriend. Get this. She's looking to extend her hours and become a work-a-holic if she can't put her free time to good use."

"How nice." Thorak replied. "Listen we're at the airport and we're about to enter our flight. Talk to you later."

"Alright, bye."

Rufus and Thorak returned to England. Back in the village of Ferlock, they were going to open their own restaurant and where Thorak would put his cooking skills to test. In secondary school he was rather a talented chef in Home Economics. (And had actually become a target of Rufus' bullying because of it.)

More time passed and Rufus and Thorak set up their restaurant. The restaurant was a huge success and people travelled miles to meet the beloved fallen boxer.

Dougal dropped in one morning to see how the restaurant was going. To his surprise, there was a huge queue all the way, round the corner. Parking spaces were filled up everywhere. There was a bouncer outside to let people in and out."

"What's all this? Is this all because of Rufus?" he asked the bouncer who was a large anthropomorphic bull.

"Clearly you haven't seen his fights dweeb, or the events he's done for charity." The bull responded in a gruff voice. "If you want in, get to the back of the line like everybody else."

"That's alright." He told the bull. "I was just leaving."

Rufus then stuck his head out of the entrance door. "Dougal, I missed you so much! It's alright Diesel, let him in."

"Whatever you say, big boss." The bouncer responded.

Dougal looked around the restaurant. There were trophies up in glass cabinets, boxing gloves hung up and newspaper articles detailing Rufus' fights. The restaurant was completely full. A television played in the background with Rufus' interviews. Although there was no sound. Subtitles played on the television.

"I'll get us a table." Rufus said to Dougal.

"But it's full." Dougal replied.

Rufus walked up to a table where a couple of two were sitting. He then got out a cheque book from his sleeveless leather jacket.

"I'll give you 10,000 gold coins if you go elsewhere to eat." He told the couple.

"Deal!" the couple both grinned.

The table was now empty. Rufus then called tor two employees to clean the table and fetch them a menu.

"How's life?" Rufus asked.

"About the same. I won't bore you. Let's talk about you." Dougal looked at Rufus' eye patch.

"Are you in any pain? How's your eye?" Dougal asked.

"I'm in no pain. But my eye is gone for good." Rufus responded.

"I'm sorry to hear." Dougal replied.

"It's okay, now we've got more in common than we think! You hated my fights, now I can't stand the idea of ever fighting again." smiled Rufus.

"Right…..We're still very different." Dougal frowned.

"So? Different doesn't mean bad." Rufus responded.

"That's not what you thought in secondary school."

"Forget what I said in school! When has harassment ever made sense? It can be done just to annoy people! It doesn't mean they hate a certain group! Leroy was a racist and used to make fun of black people and Africa in general but at the same time he loved a black comedian!"

Dougal thought it over. "I……..understand……..I think."

Rufus pointed to the menu in front of Dougal. "Pick anything from the menu. I'll pay."

"Why are you treating me like this?" Dougal asked. "We're not in some date, are we?"

"No!" Rufus asked. "Surely a friend can treat another friend to a meal."

"We're barely friends. Maybe a little more than strangers who can get along but not friends."

"You kept my boyfriend sane in childhood. That counts for something. You're sensible and….."

"I'm a NOBODY! My career goal was to be a cartoonist and a book author and I absolutely failed at both! I suffered from writer's block on a regular basis. I failed to get a book published. Aside from making a huge bunch of humorous fanfics and online stories which have received a few positive reviews and nothing else. I work part time in a supermarket and I have no ambition to be anything else. I'm…nobody."

"So you want to entertain people?" Rufus raised an eyebrow. "That's pretty admirable. You really have no inspiration for writing stories and making comics? Look around you!"

"What do you mean?"

"You're talking to a celebrity! And putting aside me, you have a girlfriend who's a sorceress and saved the world from a dictatorship!"

"Had a girlfriend. She broke up with me…..AGAIN."

"REALLY!" Rufus grinned. He then realized his mistake. "Oh…..that's a shame."

"Regardless write on her. Base a story on her, try changing the names around so you don't cause her embarrassment."

Dougal thought it over. "You…may be on to something." He spoke. "I have to have a think about it."

"Aren't you going to order something?" Rufus asked.

"Yeh. Nice try, but I'm not your sex toy. Don't cheat on Thorak." Dougal frowned.

Rufus was a bit surprised at his response.

"Still won't trust me." He sighed.

End of chapter three.

Chapter four

The following chapter is a continuation of the last chapter of my previous novel. "Amy the elf sorceress and her friends." This chapter takes place place a few months before the beginning of the story.

Amy and Misty stood outside Gerald's home beside Garrett's topless car.

"Hey Amy, me and Garrett are going to the movies, do you want to come?" Misty asked.

"Nah. I'm fine." Amy responded.

"What are you going to do today?"

"I think I'll just go for a walk." Amy smiled. "It's a nice day."

"Suit yourself." Misty replied. She got into the car and the car drove off.

Amy then headed for the park walking along the pavement, her magic book and sceptre in a small backpack she wore.

As she walked alone on a pavement. She heard loud truck horns behind her. Amy turned her head and saw a huge truck heading towards her. Inside the truck was Clobbress, a huge furry green monster with four horns and an elephant's trunk. She wore huge metal armour. She was a good friend of Phobix (the dictator that Amy had defeated in her first adventure.) and was a monster queen who had magic herself, owning an island full of monsters just off the United States. Clobbress laughed loudly as she tried to run Amy over.

Although Amy was fearless, she felt a sudden surprise just for a second. She took out her scepter and book, tossed the backpack to the side and leapt at the oncoming truck.

As she lept, she expected that the reflect spell she had cast for herself would work and that Clobbress would feel that she had been hit by a truck.

However Amy passed through the truck as if it was a hologram, she landed on the ground completely unhurt. She then turned and saw the truck disappear into nothing. Clobbress' loud laughter remained.

"What was that!?" Amy snarled to herself.

END OF CHAPTER 4

Chapter 5

One morning as Dougal was lying asleep in his bed in his flat, his phone rang. He sat up and answered it.

"Hello?" he asked rubbing his eyes. He then heard Thorak's voice.

"Dougal! It's Thorak. Rufus wants to invite you to a magic show he's holding in his restaurant."

"A magic show? I didn't see any adverts for that." Dougal asked.

"It's a practise show. He's going to see how the audience reacts to his magic before he does it for real in his restaurant."

Dougal then started to get curious. "So is Rufus just doing tricks or is he doing things with an actual magic book?"

"He has an actual magic book."

Dougal's eyes widened. His voice raised slightly. "WHERE DID HE GET THAT!?"

"In Australia before his last fight. He brought it for two million gold coins. Twice the price for one of the magic books that Gerald sells in their store. Rufus is now a magician like Amy. So will you come along? It's on Saturday at 10PM at Rufus' restaurant. After opening hours."

Dougal thought it over. "Hmmm....I dunno."

Thorak frowned. "Are you still upset he bullied you? Get over it already! He's been friendly enough to me!"

"It's not that. Magic can be dangerous in the wrong hands and it messes people up. Good magic or not."

"We've gone over the spells. There's nothing dangerous. Besides this is the village that has Amy! The sorceress that defeated Phobix! Remember?"

"Hmmm...I admit you've got a point."

"Exactly. So will you be there? I'll be there to protect you from harm if you're that scared!"

"I'll be there."

As Saturday rolled around. Dougal showed up at the restaurant. Thorak waited outside the restaurant for him.

"Glad you could make it." Thorak smiled to Dougal.

"Wouldn't miss it for the world." Dougal said in a sarcastic voice.

"Come on in." Thorak opened the door to the restaurant.

Dougal looked around the restaurant. Seated were Ralph, his talking sheep father, goblins Norman and his nephew Garrett. Gerald Woolruffe and his twin daughters Amy and Misty. There were some people that Dougal didn't know. Some were staff members of the restaurant.

Thorak introduced Dougal to a set of seats and tables. "Sit with me. The show will start soon."

Amy, Gerald and Misty sat a short distance from Dougal and Thorak. Misty then turned to Dougal.

"You've got balls showing up." Misty frowned to Dougal.

"Huh?" Dougal got confused.

"Showing your face to an event where your ex-girlfriend is."

"Sorry, I didn't know you were here and I was invited."

"You're lucky Amy and I are trained only to use fatal deadly magic in life and death situations or you'd be a frog right now. Apparently you being a big loser doesn't count." Misty smiled angrily at Dougal.

Amy then teased with Misty. "Now….now Misty, it isn't nice to make fun of people. Even if they are incredibly bland and dull with no life goals."

Dougal turned to Amy. "Why are you being so mean? You chose to break up with me. I haven't done anything to you!"

"Too right you haven't done anything!" Misty snarled. "That's the problem, you sexless freak!"

Dougal got up from his table. "Fine , I'm outta here, you obviously don't want to see me."

"Oh don't be like that." Amy smiled. "I'll actually compliment you. Out of ex-boyfriends. You're probably the most delightfully bland. 5 out of 10."

"I'll do it too. You're the most likeable loser we know. You're pathetic in a charming way." Misty grinned.

"Gee, thanks." Dougal said sarcastically rolling his eyes.

"Amy, Misty. Back off." Thorak snarled. "He's disabled, he can't help how he is."

"Alright, seriously. Enjoy the show." Amy then turned to the stage set up near the kitchen. "It'll be a nice distraction from your pathetic life."

"AMY!" Thorak snarled.

"Sorry, only meant to think that last part."

Now Gerald joined in. "Girls behave yourselves, or we'll leave."

"Alright then. No more words." Said Amy.

"Lips sealed." Smiled Misty.

Rufus then appeared from the back door. "Greeting, ladies and gentleman and welcome to my magic show! For my first trick, a display of hologrammatic fireworks that won't hurt people!"

Rufus turned on his scepter and pointed it at the ceiling. "Hologrammatic fireworks!"

Mini fireworks then shot out of Rufus' scepter. The audience was impressed enough with it.

"Oohhh….." Misty said impressed.

"I can also cure a person's eyesight and make them see well without glasses for up to 7 days! May I have a volunteer?" Rufus turned to Dougal.

"Dougal, care to volunteer?" Rufus smiled to him.

"Do it." Thorak said to Dougal elbowing him lightly.

"Fine." Dougal grumbled. He then walked up the stage. Rufus then pointed his scepter to Dougal. "Eyesight cured!"

"Whoa, blurry." Dougal said baffled. He then removed his glasses. "I…can see." He said impressed.

The audience clapped for Rufus' trick.

Thanks for being part of this trick. Can you take your seat now, Dougal?

"Sure." Dougal replied and he sat back down.

"I was told that they'd be concern about my magic tonight. To make you feel safe, I decided to cast a spell on this building for the night. If anybody hits even other with violence. The attacker will feel the pain!"

Rufus pointed his scepter to the ceiling. "Reflect building!"

The audience clapped to the spell.

"Now you won't feel any pain when I make it rain rice in here! Rice shower!"

Suddenly a huge pile of white rice fell on the audience. The audience wasn't impressed even though Rufus felt most of the pain from the rice. He was largely muscular though. Rufus still continued to smile.

"Awwww....not impressed? I can turn the rice into gold coins! Rice into gold!"

At this the rice then turned into gold coins.

"Help yourself! A little reward for showing up to my show!" Rufus grinned. "Don't get violent or you'll face the consequences of my reflect spell! Looking at you, Norman!"

"Hey!" Norman snarled.

Everybody then picked gold coins all over the restaurant. After a few more minutes of spells such as Rufus picking knotted handkerchiefs out of his ears. The magic show then came to an end.

The show had mostly been successful, although Amy had criticized that the rice into gold coins wasn't a good idea with a restaurant full of people, as people would constantly bump into each other. Rufus took Amy's advice.

"Thank you for coming to my show." Rufus shouted. "I've decided to open my bar for an hour and give half prices on all my drinks."

The audience members got up to go to the bar. Even though Dougal did like the show he just wanted to go home. Rufus noticed Dougal leaving.

"Didn't you like my show?" Rufus asked.

"It was awesome. But I don't think I should hang around longer than I should." Dougal told Rufus.

"Why not?"

"My ex-girlfriend isn't happy to see me here."

Amy then turned to Dougal. "Aww....come on, I said you were DELIGHTFULLY bland. Surely that should mean something!" she smiled.

"I don't need to be reminded I'm a failure!" Dougal snapped. "Did it ever occur I haven't TRIED to be a failure!? Despite my short attention span, I applied for several jobs never receiving a response from any of them! I work in Wesco because it was assigned to me by the National Autistic's Job Camp! And I started out at only 4 hours! I worked my way up to 16!"

At this Amy started to feel bad for what she'd said.

"In the past, I've also tried to get a book published but it got turned down everywhere and even I felt the story was stupid! Did you at least praise me for trying!?"

"Don't talk to my sister like that." Misty snarled.

Amy frowned at Misty. "Misty, stop."

"Also you're like what, only slightly better than me!? How many job offers have turned you down because they fear your magic!? How's that job as a librarian going!?"

Misty wasn't standing for that. She then took her scepter out of her backpack. Stood up from her seat and pointed her scepter at Dougal. "Mega punch!" She shouted to her scepter.

Unfortunately due to the reflect spell on the building the spell backfired. Misty threw across the room and hit her head on the wall.

"Misty!" Amy snarled. She ran to the wall only to find Misty unconscious. "Misty!" she said in a worried concerned voice.

Dougal just rolled his eyes in disbelief. "Goodbye Amy. Goodbye Misty. Don't contact me. Everybody if I show up missing or dead in the next few days. Blame these two."

Dougal then left the restaurant in a huff.

END OF CHAPTER 5

Chapter 6

Meanwhile while all this was going on. Queen Clobbress of the evil city of Bloodspike hatched a plan. Clobbress was the evil ruler of Monsterton, a country full of monsters on an island a short distance from the United States.

When Amy defeated Queen Phobix by shutting off her magic and having her city of Deathstar destroyed by the military. Amy had been interviewed for a newspaper, in it she revealed that the spell that she had used, being the only spell that could destroy a magic book could only ever be used once a year. When asked if she would ever shut off other people's magic. She revealed she would only ever do so, if the magic was used for evil. She didn't believe in ruining other people's fun with magic.

Clobbress decided to make the most of this situation and kidnap Amy's boyfriend, Dougal. To further show mow powerful she was with her magic, she resurrected Phobix, Snork and Snerk from their deaths and made them her top generals in her military. She had made the three invisible using her magic and had teleported them using her magic to gain information about Amy and blackmail her.

From what she had received. She then sent Snork, Snerk and Phobix to kidnap Dougal. Unfortunately she was unaware that they had broken up, she was a queen and a leader of the military. She had stuff to do.

With Dougal kidnapped, she would get Amy to give up her magic or else Dougal would be killed.

The next day after Rufus' magic show. Dougal woke up to hear a knocking at his flat front door.

"Who is it?" Dougal asked, hoping it wasn't Amy or Misty.

"Postman." Cried Snork's voice. "Got a package for you."

"Huh? I didn't order anything." Dougal answered the door only to get knocked out by the three villains.

He was then teleported with Snork and Snerk, Phobix put a notice through the door of Amy's home, notifying them of Dougal's kidnapping.

Dougal woke up tied to a chair in Clobbress' throne room in Monsterton. Snork and Snerk were standing near him with machine guns pointed to his head.

"He awakens." Clobbress grinned.

"What's going on. Am I dreaming?" Dougal asked.

"Nope, you're very much awake. You're the boyfriend of Amy Woolruffe aren't you?"

"More like ex-boyfriend. We broke up." Dougal replied.

At this Clobbress' smile dropped. "Uh….Are you at least good friends?"

"After last night. I don't think so." Dougal replied.

At this Clobbress then facepalmed. "Dooohhhh…."

Snerk tried to reassure Clobbress. "She might still come…."

Dougal offered a suggestion. "Maybe you should just kill me and get it over with. I thought my life was meaningless anyway."

Clobbress then snarled. "I'll decide whether you can die or not! Snork! Knock him out!"

Snork then smacked Dougal in the back of the head with his machine gun and Dougal was knocked out.

Back in Ferlock, Amy went into huge shock when she received the note. Even Misty who had been resting with an ice pack on her head from the previous night thought Dougal's kidnapping was immoral.

"We can't give up our magic. Don't forget Phobix nearly destroyed a city by meteors once." Amy told Misty.

"Dougal may have his flaws but he was still a generally nice man. We can't let him die." Misty panicked. "Plus if we use our magic to destroy the monsters, they'll probably shoot him on sight."

"That's not all, according to the note, Clobbress can cancel any spells we use on ourselves, so we can't use that reflect spell on ourselves." Amy gritted her teeth in fear.

"Maybe....maybe....there's one person who can help us." Misty offered.

"Who?" Amy asked.

"Rufus."

Chapter 7

Showing up at Rufus' restaurant. Amy and Misty demanded to see the manager. When they were denied access. They used their magic to teleport themselves just outside Rufus' office.

Amy knocked on the door for Rufus' office. And Rufus answered.

"How did you get in here?" Rufus answered.

"They'll be time for explanations later. Dougal's been kidnapped!" Amy shouted.

Rufus went into shock. "What!? By whom!?"

"Queen Clobbress." Misty answered.

"She demands that we give up our magic or else Dougal will be killed!" Amy cried. "We can't do that! Her destructive magic will destroy the world!"

"Do you have any magic that could help us?" asked Misty.

Rufus thought it over. "Yes, I think I do."

"We need to work together!" cried Amy. "With all three of us , Dougal will be safe!"

"Don't you hate each other, right now?" Rufus asked.

"Well…..uh…kinda….but we can't let him die. If he dies what will stop more innocent people being kidnapped and murdered?" Amy struggled.

"She's got a point there." Misty replied.

"I'll save Dougal…..by myself. You two have done enough to him." Rufus closed his eyes.

"I think he'll forgive us if we save his life!" Misty snarled.

"And then what, you'll talk for a bit and then break up again." Rufus frowned.

"Heyyy…..relationships are complicated. We'll work it out!" Amy growled.

"I'll save him, by myself." Rufus pointed to himself.

"Ha! I doubt your magic is better than ours." Amy said smugly.

"Shall I show you? I promise you'll come to no harm." Rufus grinned. He then went and got his magic book out of a drawer at his work desk.

"What have you got?" Misty asked.

Rufus pointed his scepter to the ceiling. "FREEZE TIME!" Immediately time stopped and Rufus was the only one able to move.

He then took Amy and Misty's spell books and read them over. Using their magic, he then teleported to Monsterton, picked up Dougal (still tied to a chair) and teleported him back. But not before removing Clobbress' and Queen Phobix's clothes and putting them in the middle of a city which would make them naked to many monsters. Many monsters would be able to see their naughty parts.

Queen Clobbress didn't have breasts. But Rufus had removed her armour and shaved her green fur, humiliating her all the same.

He then returned to his restaurant, gave back Amy and Misty's spell books and restored time.

"I've got that!" he smiled.

Amy and Misty then went into shock at seeing Dougal alive. Rufus had placed a sleeping spell on him as he figured he'd be in too much shock if he just suddenly found himself in another room.

Misty widened her eyes in shock. "How did you do that!?"

"I'll explain later." Rufus smiled. "Magic, teleport Amy and Misty along with their magic books to their home."

Amy's scepter who had still been turned on teleported the sisters and their magic away.

"God...sneaking into my office." He snarled. "What creeps."

Dougal still tied to the chair was woken up by Rufus. Dougal looked around and noticed Rufus.

"What's going on now?" he asked.

"You're back home in Ferlock now." Rufus revealed. "You were kidnapped but I saved your life."

Dougal was baffled. "Wait....I was rescued by.....YOU!?"

"Yes. Thank god you're safe." At this Rufus gave Dougal a big hug. A tear dropped from his eye in happiness.

"Just why!? I didn't realize I was that important of a sex toy to you! Are you really that horny!?" shouted Dougal.

"You don't have to have sex with me!" shouted Rufus. "I'm just glad you're safe!" still hugging Dougal tightly.

Dougal's ex bully had now saved his life. Now eternally grateful for Rufus' heroism. Dougal FINALLY learned to forgive Rufus and see him as a friend.

Did they become boyfriends? Well....no. Dougal may have had a muscle fetish (and also a fat fetish), but despite his fetishes. He still had common sense. Rufus was way bigger than him and would have crushed him if they ever shared a bed together or had sex together. Being crushed by big dragon pecs in the face wasn't worth it.

Also relationships were complicated. And Dougal knew they would be arguments in any relationship. Dougal had heard about dragons who had set each other on fire when they had a falling out. Despite Rufus making promises that he would never do that. Dougal wasn't sure.

In response to the kidnapping. Dougal stayed at Rufus' bigger house. Where he was looked after.

Despite them not being lovers that didn't stop both Amy and Thorak from getting jealous. Despite pretending to not be jealous. They were ways that it showed.

One time while Dougal was watching television. Thorak showed up wearing a sleeveless leather jacket asking if Rufus would love to see him in it and that he'd try a more bad boy look.

Showing no signs of hesitation. Dougal just told him he'd look great in it, which confused Thorak.

After returning to his flat, declaring it was safe. A day later. Amy showed up sobbing her eyes and apologized for how she'd been to Dougal and that she hoped Rufus would make him happy.

Dougal just stared blankly thinking. "Uh….what?"

And what became of Queen Clobbress and her generals, Phobix ? Well that's a story for another time…..

Chapter 8

Meanwhile back in Australia, Sharker the boxer dragon was proud of his victory and was proud to be the most undefeated boxer ever. One day in his home, he decided to get comments from his latest fans on Facebook.

To his shock much of the feedback was negative. Much of it was frowning how he had ruined one of the nicest boxers , scolding how he had permanently ruined someone's eyesight and that there were accusations that he had cheated the fight. Despite no proof.

"Ahhh…..nuts." Sharker sighed.

End of chapter 8.

Chapter 9

The next day after Amy had met up with Dougal, Amy rang the doorbell at Rufus' huge home.

"Hey, what's up?" Rufus answered.

"I just want to thank you for saving Dougal, even though it wasn't quite as planned. I'm grateful that you saved him."

"No problem , are you back to being boyfriend and girlfriend."

"Uhhh...not really, after Dougal explained that you and him weren't a couple. I kinda mocked I wasn't that desperate to get back with him."

Rufus folded his arms in disgust. "You're unbelievable."

"I know. I know. I suck. But he can't meet my expectations."

"And what do you want in a man?" asked Rufus.

"I want someone successful who makes enough for me to own a house with, someone who isn't a pushover, someone tough but also kind and considerate and most of all someone who isn't afraid of my magic."

Rufus thought it over. "I think I might know someone. Care to come in?"

Amy got puzzled. "Uh…..what?"

"Just come in, I'll just talk about somebody I know who might be perfect for you. It's perfectly up to you if you want to date him or not."

Amy decided to go along with it. She came in and sat in Rufus' huge living room. A butler had served her a cola and Rufus had already discussed his plan with her. He had talked to her about dating a big green orc by the name of Vulgarth Grogmark.

"You want me to date a wrestler?" Amy raised an eyebrow.

"Outside his wrestling, he's a nice guy, and he makes tons of money in his fights." Rufus explained.

"How do you a boxer know a wrestler?" Amy asked.

"A bit of a crossover, when he was a kid he practised boxing as well as wrestling, and he wanted a boxing match with me. I won of course. But he appreciated the match and gave me a phone number if I ever wanted to talk with him."

"What make you think he'll be interested in dating me? He probably has girls who'll never leave him alone."

"Well like you he's talented in magic, and has a magic book too and along with it a similar problem to you, many women are turned off by his magic."

"He knows magic too!? Amazing!"

"Yes, he actually has a YouTube channel where he performs harmless magic tricks."

"How can I get in touch with him?" Amy grinned.

"I'll call him right now, he lives in a big house in Canada and does occasional fights in Canada."

Rufus dialled his mobile phone. "Hello Vulgarth? It's Rufus Silverclaw Oakhoof. Yeah….that's my full name…..I was adopted by a centaur that's why! Listen I have a sorceress who might be interested in meeting you. Can you teleport to here? She'd love to meet you. I live in a big house in England."

Suddenly a tall muscular but also slightly overweight orc teleported to the room. Despite being an orc, he had a cute face with long black hair and a beard. All he worn was a pair of jeans and some sandals.

Rufus was disgusted. "Put a shirt on in front of a woman!" he shouted.

"I......don't mind." Amy swooned.

Time passed, Vulgarth explained where he originally came from. He was originally from an island from Orcland a small island a short distance off Canada. It was not to be confused with two other islands orc populated islands Orcville and Orcworld. Orcville was an island where 630 years ago, it was an island with a population of 5 million, a short distance from France, they had tried to conquer Europe with their dark magic. Unfortunately, it had not gone as planned. Europe had fought back with magic of their own. Upon losing over 75% of the population of Orcville, the island surrendered.

It was there that orcs decided to change their ways and stop being evil bloodthirsty monsters. Orcland and Orcworld had picked up on what happened to Orcville and changed their ways too. Orcland however was an island of only 10 thousand in the year 992 and in the year 1622 it was an island of only around 50 thousand, many had left to seek fortune outside the island. Orcworld had twice the population of Orcland and like Orcland many had left their island to seek fortune.

Orcland and Orcworld were a bit like developing islands. Education wasn't compulsory (but it was in Orcville) and Vulgarth had only attended school in Orcland for about 6 years. He had never attended high school and had been wrestling and boxing since he was 12 years old, wrestling in teenage orc tournaments around the world aimed at young orcs like him to help raise money for his family. Orcs loved to fight (even the females) and many of them had gone into fighting careers such as boxing or wrestling. When he turned 18 he enrolled into worldwide wrestling that didn't have all opponents as orcs. He was only 23 years old. 3 years younger than Amy.

Vulgarth had been involved in many charity events donating much of his winning money to poor countries and not just his own. This attracted Amy to Vulgarth even more.

They started dating and despite Vulgarth's ignorance towards certain subjects, Amy just found his naïve behaviour adorable.

Amy started living with Vulgarth, checking in on occasion on her family and old friends. Time passed unlike her previous dates, she had stuck with Vulgarth for several months and it soon became known that they would marry.

Upon asking Misty and Thorak how Dougal was doing. Misty hadn't been seeing Dougal herself because of her relationship with Garrett. Misty had informed that Dougal was just the same as he had always been. He was still working minimum wage in a supermarket with little thought on his future. According to Thorak. He wasn't socializing much. Having little care that all his friends and family and moving on were now in relationships while he was all alone.

That made Amy feel somewhat sad for Dougal and guilty for how she had treated him.

Amy being a powerful sorceress was unpopular in school.

Dougal was Amy's few childhood friends and being his neighbour only three houses down they had grew up together. Even though Dougal didn't find Amy sexually attractive. They had lots of great memories together. They had read and discussed manga and comics with each other. Seen movies and helped each other in learning certain subjects in secondary school. Had many entertaining conversations with each other. They had played video games with each other many times. If they couldn't be boyfriend and girlfriend. Could they at least be good friends? Despite not being lovers she actually missed him. In school he had been one of Amy's few friends.

Despite how Amy was not allowed to take magic books to school. Many were terrified of her magic. She could always cast spells on herself before she left the house. Dougal however was one of the few fascinated by her magic and was one of the few students who was a human. He had his own problems with fitting in and so was his dragon brother, Thorak.

More memories came back about how Dougal used to help Thorak with his poor grades. Although Thorak never got higher than a B on a few subjects. With many of his subjects getting B's to C-'s. Dougal had helped Thorak tackle many subjects he had difficulty with and improved his grades. Amy herself sometimes needed help and vice versa.

Memories came with how Amy and her friends were referred to as the "five oddballs" in school.

Both Amy and her sister Misty were unpopular due to their magic, Dougal due to being a human, Thorak to being a dragon and unintelligent at times, and Garrett for being a short goblin with a temper problem. Later on in secondary school though, Thorak had been shown to be good at sports and became more popular. He joined a tennis club and made more friends. He did still stick up for Dougal though.

"I gotta help him." Amy thought to herself.

End of Chapter 9

Chapter 10

Amy felt bad for Dougal's lack of success. He worked in a supermarket stocking shelves. He wasn't a cartoonist nor a book author as he had always dreamed. As he had stated he had applied for several jobs never receiving a response from any of them. He had never been in a job interview. Working in a supermarket as a result of a company that helped autistic people back into work.

Amy missed Dougal's kindness. She told Vulgarth in his Canadian home that she would be visiting him.

"You're going to visit your ex-boyfriend? Are you nuts? Is this some sort of joke?" Vulgarth snarled at Amy.

"You've got nothing to worry about. He's an asexual. He hasn't got a sex drive." Amy told Vulgarth.

Vulgarth smiled. "Heh…really?" He then grinned. "How pathetic."

"Pathetically adorable. And that's why I miss him."

"You have a deal on one condition. I come with."

"Alright, but I swear you have nothing to worry about."

"Best be safe."

Vulgarth and Amy used their magic to teleport to the village of Ferlock, England.

Amy knocked on the front of Dougal's door to his flat.

"Who is it?" Dougal asked.

"Amy."

"You!? Have you come to mock me!?" Dougal growled.

"Yes." Vulgarth teased.

Amy elbowed Vulgarth in the chest. "Stop it! No I haven't, Dougal. Please let's just talk. That's all. Please open your door."

"What's there to talk about?" Dougal opened his door.

"I want to remain friends with you. I've missed you too much."

"Remain friends, why?"

"Maybe it's your intelligence, your kindness and your adorable nerd face."

"And yet you're now dating a wrestler."

"I grew bored with you and you weren't able to keep plans for a future together. It happens. Doesn't mean we can't be friends."

"You'll just mock that I'm a failure." Dougal frowned.

"Maybe I can help you. Don't you have any big plans for your life. Have you applied for any new jobs?"

"We've gone over this before. My only goal is to be a cartoonist and a book author. Rufus suggested I do a story based off you and change names. But I'm not cold hearted enough to humiliate you."

Amy thought it over. "He might be on to something there. It wouldn't be humiliating."

Dougal raised his eyebrows. "You sure?"

Moments later, Amy, Dougal and Vulgarth sat in Dougal's furniture in his flat. They discussed how to make the story different enough from their everyday lives.

As a result "Mega Magic Heroic Princess Elven Twins." was born.

The story starred two twin elven sisters who were princesses of a kingdom in a fantasy universe called Mega Earth. The princesses were twins called Ada and Mavis Woolton and they lived in a city populated by mostly elves called Elfville. Ada being the oldest and Mavis the youngest. The twins were well talented sorceresses and their kingdom was at war with the evil populated orc kingdom Orctropolis ruled by their evil orc queen Clawdia.

The story revolved around evil Clawdia making many attempts to conquer Elfville being stopped by the two elven sisters every time. After many failed attempts Ada developed a spell that could shut off magic. Upon shutting off Clawdia's magic and leaving them powerless. Ada sent her (non robot) army to defeat Clawdia once and for all, with help from the magic she had developed of her own.

Peace reigned forever and despite the mother of the elf sorceresses frowning that they did not marry princes. Ada married a human (who actually had a sex drive and was more successful) while Mavis married a bad tempered but well meaning muscular goblin. (clearly based on Garrett.)

Dougal wrote the text with help from Amy and Dougal provided the illustrations with help from Amy too.

The forty-chapter book was published by help of Amy and Vulgarth. As Vulgarth was already a huge celebrity there had been little problems in publishing the book.

Although Dougal's one story didn't make him a millionaire. He was satisfied that he had accomplished his dream goal once and for all. Dougal finally learned to forgive Amy for her flaws and look at her as a friend.

"Thank you." Dougal hugged Amy one day just outside Vulgarth's home in Canada.

"That's okay. I couldn't leave you to be alone forever. I can't promise that you'll become rich just by selling a story. Plus I can't help but wonder that some of the ideas that we used were just hilariously bad."

"It's okay, I write to entertain not for money. Plus have you ever seen fanfiction? Tons of people pay attention to purposely hilariously bad fanfiction and never any attention to good fanfiction. As long as what I write is entertaining and doesn't anger lots of people. It's okay with me."

Dougal went home to England while Amy and Vulgarth remained in Canada.

END OF CHAPTER 10.

Chapter 11

Dougal continued his job as a customer assistant for Wesco. Although he was not a millionaire, he could be happy he had less money problems making a third of the sales off his book. Through permission he allowed Amy and Vulgarth to continue the stories of the characters he wrote in his book but was not involved in what direction the characters were taken. He made no money on the books written but did not mind.

Amy and Vulgarth settled down in Canada while Vulgarth continued to wrestle. They never had kids as Amy believed that their magic was too powerful and not suitable for child's hands.

One of her spells the spell that allowed her to shut off people's magic was actually taken away from her. The Prime Minister of Sweden, a powerful magician made a proposal to take the spell away from her to risk her becoming a heartless, ruthless dictator. 62% of Sweden voted yes and through magic the spell was taken away from her and destroyed.

Misty and Garrett had kids though. After Amy dated Vulgarth, Garrett took Amy's place in her flat. They settled down and had a son. Keep in mind Misty was half-human, half-elf and Garrett was a goblin. They gave birth to a human, elf and goblin hybrid…which didn't look so bad. They would keep from using magic until the child was old enough.

Thorak and Rufus settled down in their home too. Rufus continued to be successful in his restaurant.

Snork, Snerk, Phobix and Clobberess had difficulty making plans for world domination due to being humiliated by Rufus. For now, they would keep their destructive plans to themselves.

END OF BOOK THREE.

BOOK FOUR

Dougal's non-contagious werewolf girlfriend

Chapter 1

And now, let's begin the fourth book in the Clastonia series.

Shortly after Dougal's first book was published. Although Amy believed that she could maintain contact with Dougal, this wasn't the case. Even though Dougal couldn't get erections, he still had feelings for Amy. And not only would he just get jealous of Amy hanging out with Vulgarth, he figured that Vulgarth wouldn't want to see him too.

When Amy called Dougal inviting him to a trip out. Dougal turned it down explaining his situation.

Considering that Vulgarth would get annoyed when Amy told Vulgarth of her childhood memories with Dougal. Amy began to get a clue.

She had lost one of her few childhood friends. The one of the few people who wasn't intimidated by her magic. That hurt.

As a result they stopped contacting each other. Amy sobbed at how horrible she'd been.

A year passed, two more books had been published without Dougal's involvement. The first one had sold well due to a famous wrestler being involved in publishing it and promoting it.

Despite Dougal having no involvement and the illustrations being done by another artist. The books had sold well.

More time passed and another year passed. Amy and Vulgarth had gotten married. Dougal hadn't been invited to the wedding. Only Amy's father, Gerald, her sister Misty and her boyfriend and new born son were invited to the wedding. They had left Dougal and his side of the family out due to jealously issues.

During all this time Dougal just kept himself to himself. He was autistic after all. Although he wasn't anti-social and did socialize with people at work, and occasionally with Thorak and his adopted talking sheep father Ralph. He was very quiet and often kept his thoughts to himself, often being afraid he'd say the wrong thing to someone.

In his spare time while all his friends had moved on. Dougal would read comics and manga, watch Youtube videos and play video games. On occasion he would read fanfiction and watch the occasional movie often battling his short autistic attention span while doing so. He would pause and stop movies, go do something else and then come back and finish it.

"Nice and boring." Dougal smiled thinking to himself. "Maybe it wouldn't be acceptable in a sitcom. But in the real world it's somewhat acceptable. And peaceful too."

Although Dougal had only dated Amy. He never made any attempts to date anybody else. Not just because of being asexual. But because he was too afraid of getting rejected. As well as Amy, he'd seen how people got rejected on TV shows and the fiction that he read.

"People are mean plus relationships are too complicated." He thought. "Just let me be a gloomy boring bastard in peace. Last thing I want is to be the kind of loser who repeatedly dates and can't stick with a girlfriend."

Despite all this, in his time, he would occasionally write fanfiction and he also often thought about writing another story. Like his first story, it would be written entirely by him. (Well, he wrote at least most of the first one. But this time it would be 100% his words.) Maybe he could steer away from high fantasy for once and leave magic out of it. Maybe he could watch and read more serious things for inspiration battling his short attention span and watching and reading this stuff all the way to the end.

"Why not?" he thought. "It'll take time but I'll manage. You only live once. Plus nobody cares enough to resurrect me."

In the time passed, the authors of the books Amy and Vulgarth and later Misty had been interviewed by a number of sources. Misty had later got involved with writing the third and fourth book. Dougal wasn't present for any of the interviews. Amy, Vulgarth and later Misty had shown up for them and Amy had stated that she had done the first book in favour of a childhood friend. A very special friend who had helped her keep her sanity. And that she hoped that he would forgive her and keep in touch at least sometimes. Dougal had done nearly all the writing of the first book. Vulgarth and Amy had just given him a couple of ideas and checked his grammar. Dougal did believe in being fair and giving Amy and Vulgarth credit in the writing in his book.

Through the interviews people started to get curious who Dougal was. Through the interviews he was just a man who showed up to write one book before disappearing in the shadows. He had no Facebook page. Attempts to contact him had been minimal. He had received PM's through his FanFiction page. Although he just ignored them.

The reason for this was that he didn't want anything remotely related to Amy in his life again. He had moved on.

"A boring silent loner nobody with few words. That's me." Dougal smiled to himself one day while leaving the flat one day for his supermarket job. "Who needs to be famous anyway? How many famous people ruin their lives with drugs anyway?" Just as he left his home. He was surprised to find several reporters standing outside with microphones at his face.

"Hi." A talking grey haired squirrel with black hair said to him holding a microphone to his face. "Care to talk?"

"Uh....." Dougal struggled.

"Where do you get your inspiration from?"

"Several video games plus...."

"Do you have plans for a new book?"

"Maybe, in time I'm..."

"Misty said you have a curse where you can shoot harmless rockets out your arse. Is that true?"

"She said WHAT!?"

"Suddenly Amy, Misty and a third girl who Dougal didn't recognize teleported and appeared behind Dougal in the corridor. The third girl looked like a Japanese human who had red hair in pigtails.

"Everybody back off!" Amy shouted. "Give the author some breathing room! You hurt Dougal, you answer to us! We're powerful sorceresses!"

"We've told you everything you need to know about Dougal. Back off and leave him alone!" Misty snarled.

Dougal just stared blankly. "What the hell's going on!?" He thought.

"Get out of here!" yelled the third red haired Japanese girl. "Don't make me turn wolf on you!"

"Who's she!?" thought Dougal. "Turn wolf what?"

The crowd muttered words of disapproval and slowly they backed off.

"What just happened?" Dougal turned to Amy.

"Sorry Dougal, we tried to make the reporters leave you alone. But the fact that we grew up in the same hometown did not help matters." Amy replied.

Amy then turned to Misty. "Somebody had to say our hometown accidently during an interview!" Amy snarled.

Misty put up her hands in defence. "I'm sorry!" she said nervously.

"Er....I guess I should say, thanks for helping." Dougal suggested.

"You're welcome." At this Amy then hugged him tightly. "Oh, it's been so long. I missed you so much!"

"Where the hell have you been!?" Misty asked. "You've made barely any contact with anybody! Even Thorak, Rufus and your dad say they barely see you!"

Dougal struggled for words. "We broke up! And I know being her sister you'd try to hurt me if I tried to contact you!" Dougal snarled.

"Amy told me not to! Well, maybe just a little! Don't ignore your friends!" Misty growled.

Amy stopped hugging Dougal and Dougal then turned his eyes to the Japanese red-haired girl. "And who's this girl?"

"I'm Takara." Replied the Japanese girl. "Surely you've watched my magic tricks on YouTube?"

Dougal didn't have the heart to tell her that he refused to have anything to do with sorceresses again because it reminded him too much of the times he had with Amy.

"Uhhhhh…..no." he said simply.

"I reviewed your book! It's how I met Amy and became friends! She told me all about you. She always admired how tolerant and accepting you were of magic and how you always cheered her up when she was down. You were such a good friend to her. And to Misty as well."

"But I wasn't a good lover and a hard worker so Amy left me." Dougal frowned. "I wish you luck in your new life, but leave me out of it."

Amy put her arm around Dougal's shoulder. "Oh…..c'mon let's catch up, be friends like old times. Takara's wanted to interview you."

"There's nothing to say. I'm a gloomy boring bastard and that's all you need to know. Let me be Eeyore the donkey in human form in peace."

"You're not boring! You make awesome stories! Your fanfiction and one book is hilarious!" Takara frowned. "C'mon please…. take a day off work and talk to us…please."

"Even I've missed you!" Misty begged. "Do I need to give you the puppy dog eyes?"

Amy, Misty and Takara tried to make puppy dog eye looks at Dougal.

"Fine." Dougal sighed.

After booking a day off work. Dougal, Amy, Misty and Takara sat in Dougal's flat. Dougal had poured some glasses of cola for his guests.

"Tell us a bit about yourself." Takara started. "I've been wanting to meet you!"

"What else do you want be to say? I'm looking for inspiration and I'm looking at more serious things battling my short attention span doing so. I failed in my goal of being a cartoonist. I failed at getting better jobs and it drove Amy away. Even today I still don't have much inspiration for getting better jobs. All I want is to write stories and entertain people. I don't care for fame. I don't care for the money."

Takara just stared blankly thinking over at what Dougal had just said. "You love to entertain people! That's so adorable! Admirable!"

"Look even though you didn't seek it. Over time you've become a celebrity." Amy frowned. "Even though you didn't write the sequels. People want to know you. You've become famous."

"It'll go away in time." Dougal frowned.

"In the meantime, people want and love your ass. Maybe you should keep Takara around as a bodyguard." Misty pointed to Takara.

Takara pointed to herself. "I'll do an awesome job. I'm a werewolf who can turn into a huge muscular wolf anytime I want. I lose control of my human form every time there's a full moon though."

Dougal then immediately raised his eyebrows. His eyes widened. "WAIT! WHAT!?"

Misty enjoyed seeing Dougal panicked. "You heard her. She's a werewolf."

"And you think she should be a bodyguard for me!?" said a now scared Dougal.

"Yeh...what's the problem? I retain most of my personality in my wolf form, plus I'm non-contagious."

"What? A....non-contagious werewolf? Surely there's no such thing."

"I'm sorry Dougal. I should explain better. There have been four types of magic werewolf curses discovered. I just happen to have one where the curse isn't spread by biting and attacking."

"Four types of magic werewolf curses?" Dougal frowned.

"Yeh....where do you think werewolves originated from?" Amy asked.

"Some sort of virus?" Dougal offered.

"What kind of virus makes people ill on a full moon? A magic curse makes more sense!" Amy frowned.

"You so stupid!" Misty teased.

"Yeh, in history there's been four different types of werewolf curse discovered." Takara explained. A non-contagious one, a contagious one, one contagious where you lose your personality and become a snarling beast. And one where you turn into a literal wolf. Not a wolf beast. A non-talking literal wolf. It's designed to humiliate the enemy."

"Humiliate?" asked Dougal.

"Yeh…in real life wolves attacking people have happened. But they're rare. Most wolves run away at the sight of people. They're very shy beautiful animals." Takara continued.

"Just imagine having a new girlfriend." Amy smiled. "Maybe we could hang out again as friends, Dougal!"

"Takara's nice. Give her a chance. " Misty grinned.

Dougal just face palmed. "Let me spare you a hard break up. I'm not boyfriend material."

Takara didn't back down. "Sure you are. Everybody is. Even drug addicts date other drug addicts."

"I'll tell you some things that'll put you off. I have no sex drive. I'm asexual."

"I've become more horny as a werewolf. Maybe we can turn you into one!"

Dougal's eyes widened again. " YOU'LL DO NO SUCH THING! "

Takara put up her hands in defence. "I kid. I kid. But seriously Amy told me you used Viagra. We'll do that."

"I make minimum wage working 16 hours in a supermarket. I have a short attention span and no interest for other jobs. Other ways of money, I make off books."

"I work as a waitress in both a flower shop and café for 12 hours a week. I wanted to be a model and I failed at that. I make additional money selling super cheap microwaves I can make by magic and through a patreon account by making YouTube videos."

"Er….wow." Dougal replied. "Okay, how about it's okay if you eat Japanese food, but I'm not a big fan of it?"

"Hey, you eat whatever."

Suddenly a loud voice came outside Dougal's flat. "Mr Dougal are you back? Please do an interview!"

"Oh no, more reporters!" Dougal gulped.

"I'll sort this out." Takara got up and went to Dougal's bedroom. She then opened up the window and yelled.

"I'm interviewing him. Everybody back off and look for my interview with him on my YouTube channel! Back off or face powerful magic! I'm a sorceress!"

Dougal then came to the bedroom window and Takara put his arm around him. "Mess with Dougal. You mess with me!"

The reporters then again made mutters of disapproval and slowly backed off. When they were out of sight. Takara then turned to Dougal.

"See…..you need me. They're gonna come back."

"No! I don't want to get heartbroken again!" Dougal groaned.

"Tell you what." Takara smiled. "We'll just be friends for now. No kissing, no sleeping together. I'll just protect you till the heat's off, okay? Then we don't have to talk again."

Dougal thought it over. "I guess…..that's okay."

Amy hugged Dougal. "Yay! We can be friends again!"

Misty hugged Dougal also. "Yay…..someone I can play pranks on again!"

Takara took a photo selfie of herself and Dougal and teleported back to Japan with her magic to do her video on how she had meet Dougal. She made both a Japanese and a English version of the video. A few days later, she filmed herself actually talking to Dougal. Dougal went through with the interview thinking it would get people to back off. The video made a news article.

"The creator of "Mega Magic Heroic Princess Elven Twins" resurfaces!"

Takara stayed with Dougal for a bit. To show manners, Takara would sleep in Dougal's bed while he would sleep on the couch. Despite Takara insisting that Dougal sleep with her. Dougal wanted to stick with his "Just friends" policy.

End of Chapter 1

Chapter 2

One night Takara shared her childhood stories with Dougal in his kitchen and living room. Growing up in Japan, she was not bitten by another werewolf but had voluntarily transformed herself into a werewolf to make other kids fear her and to prevent people bullying her. She wanted to be a tough but friendly person to all. Similar to Amy she had few friends. Her other two friends were a yellow dragon named Rosetta and a female jackalope named Hanami.

"Rosetta? Doesn't sound very Japanese." Dougal replied.

"Her parents thought she looked beautiful like a flower. Plus she has Italian ancestors." Takara explained. "Say…what's the moon out tonight."

Dougal went to his bedroom and looked outside. "Pretty full but not completely full." He said in relief.

Suddenly a loud magic noise was heard. POOF! It sounded like.

"The curse still works if the moon is mostly full." Takara said. Dougal gulped.

Dougal then walked back to his living room only to see a large muscular now naked brown wolf beast on his couch.

Up to now Takara had kept from showing Dougal her wolf form. Takara's body looked masculine. She had no breasts. Her red hair in pigtails still remained.

"WHOA!" Dougal said shocked.

Takara patted Dougal's couch with her now huge claw. "Come and sit next to me. I love how tame your game shows are in this country."

Dougal didn't argue with the now huge wolf beast. After sitting with Takara, Takara then put her large now furry arm around Dougal. Dougal gulped nervously.

"You're so cute, we've got so much in common you and me." Takara smiled a huge fanged smile at Dougal. "We both love to have fun a lot. We both don't like working really long hours in our jobs."

"True." Dougal just stared blankly at the television nervous.

"Even asexuals can have sex you know. You must have some kind of fetish. Some have fetishes for anthropomorphic animals, muscles, obesity, pregnancy the list is endless. You have to jerk off to something or you'd be full of testosterone. You don't act angry all the time."

"Uhhh….." Dougal struggled.

While Dougal actually DID have a muscle and a fat fetish. In real life he would never actually HAVE sex with a muscular or an obese person. For muscles. He thought that he would mostly be intimated by their large size and he was afraid with how the partner would control him. Being intimidated did not turn him on.

For obesity, he was aware that being obese was supposed to be a bad thing and that it killed people. In real life, eating unhealthy non-stop and being obese in real life killed people and he would never want to have a girlfriend like that. Plus stuffing people to kill them would just be seen as disgusting in real life.

Also depending on how large the fat or muscle is. There would be the possibility he would be crushed to death in his sleep. And being dead meant no video games.

Being killed over sex was not something he wanted. That was why he didn't get together with Rufus. He thought many times of what might come after death.

He wasn't sure if there was a heaven or a hell, and if they existed if he was good enough to go to heaven. What if he went to hell? Was there such a thing as reincarnation? He read articles on the internet that there was proof of reincarnation. He wondered if they were true or not. If they were. What if he was reincarnated as somebody who would live an even worse life than he already lived?

Whatever he was reincarnated as, he'd have to face school again, that sucked. Or worse, what if he was reincarnated in a poverty stricken country that had war in it?

Probably the worst thing about death is that he'd just see black forever. Nothingness. But even so he wanted to live for the positive things in life.

Would Takara crush him? She was now huge, but not too huge. Being a werewolf would she even be impressed by his penis?

"I've thought you were cute for so long. Have sex with me." Takara grinned at Dougal.

"W-WH-WHAT!?" Dougal screamed in fear.

"I won't bite. Honest!" Takara grinned a fanged smile at Dougal.

Dougal gritted his teeth in fear. "Er…..I'll need the Viagra."

"You still don't find me sexually attractive. Pathetic. You know how many people I've had sex with in this form? I'll admit they aren't humans. But my point still stands.

"I told you! I'm ASEXUAL!" Dougal panicked. He then realized something then smiled. "Plus my bed only takes one person!"

Takara rolled her eyes. "Fine, we'll use my bed." She then took her magic sceptre and flicked it on. "Teleport me and Dougal to my flat in Japan!"

Dougal and Takara teleported to Takara's flat in Japan. Takara's flat was well decorated and large. Takara then went to a large bed big enough for three humans.

Dougal just shook in fear. So much was happening. Takara then noticed his terrified expression. She then softened.

"Awww...you poor thing. You're so scared. Fine.....we'll do things the easy way, get that extra large buzzing dildo out of the drawer next to this bed."

Dougal went to the drawer and opened it, he then got a huge dildo out of the drawer.

"NOW WORK!"

Dougal carried out his order of sexual acts on Takara. After Takara had received an orgasm, Takara then grinned at Dougal. "Now c'mon and cuddle me! We'll have a nap together!"

Dougal then got into Takara's bed and Takara put her hairy arms around him. "Mmmm....your skin's so smooth! And you're so small! Thanks for your wonderful time. I'd been horny for you for so long!"

"Err…..no problem." Dougal said nervously. He had no problem but to sleep with Takara. Luckily for Dougal this was only for a few hours. It had been around 8pm spring time in Britain when Takara had transformed. In Japan it was 4AM. A few hours later it was daytime making Takara transform back into her human form. Maybe Takara would go easy on him now.

"Hey, wake up." Dougal said quietly to Takara.

Takara awakened only to get a sudden shock. "Dougal, why are you in my bed!?"

"You transformed into a werewolf and forced me to have sex with you!" shouted Dougal.

"I….DID WHAT!?" Takara jumped in fright. "Oh my god! Dougal, I'm so sorry!"

"Does the full moon make you extra horny!?" Dougal snapped at Takara.

"It actually does." Takara replied simply. "Plus I hadn't had sex for so long. I guess I got a little drunk with power. I'm really sorry."

Dougal just wondered what to make of all this. This was undoubtedly RAPE. Could he tell the police whether in Japan or Britain any of this? And even if the police took him seriously, how could Takara get arrested? She was a powerful sorceress from Japan after all. Plus if Dougal broke up with her, would she even stay away from him? Despite what she'd done. Takara still seemed like a mostly harmless werewolf. Rape on men was still different. At least there was no risk of becoming pregnant.

"If you like you can get me back." Takara smiled. "How about I turn you into a werewolf and we have a wrestling match?"

Dougal thought it over. "Revenge is not an answer. Plus we've talked this over. I prefer to stay human."

"We live in a world full of talking animals and creatures such as dragons, ogres, elves, goblins and all sorts of creatures and where humans are a rare species! Why do you think being a werewolf is a bad thing!?"

"I don't need to intimidate anybody! Plus I'll still freak people out every time there's a full moon! Plus I do work nights in a supermarket! What will my boss say about me turning into a wolf!?"

"He'll get over it! You'll have super strength! The ability to breathe ice beams and lightening! And immunity to many diseases!"

"You can breathe what!? I'm dating a Pokémon now!?"

"Yeh, I can do that. Oddly enough only the non-contagious werewolves are reported to do that. So will you become a werewolf?"

"Still no. Drop the subject. Can you teleport me home to England now, please?"

"Sure thing. Are we still dating?" Takara asked.

"Er….sure." Dougal said simply thinking he had no choice in the matter.

Dougal was teleported home to England.

Despite Takara finally being able to have sex with Dougal. She wasn't satisfied. She wanted large werewolf cock and an actual horny Dougal. She needed to find a way to turn Dougal into a werewolf. She knew she couldn't force Dougal by turning him into a werewolf without her permission, as well as it being immoral, and that Dougal probably could kill her in revenge. Amy had a spell to undo magic spells and curses cast.

Werewolves could fight off many diseases. Maybe she could make Dougal incredibly sick to the point of dying. And that turning him into a werewolf could possibly fight his disease.

She decided to ask Amy and Misty for help...

END OF CHAPTER 2

Chapter 3

The next day Takara met up with the sisters Amy and Misty in Canada, and they spent part of the day sitting a table outside a posh coffee shop and café in Canada. Takara met the sisters in her human form.

"How are things with Dougal?" Amy asked.

"This should be a laugh." Misty smiled.

"He's a nice guy, but good god he's dull. He's not even that good at sex!" Takara sighed.

"I knew it!" Misty closed her eyes and grinned.

"Misty , enough!" Amy snarled.

"Err….no offense, but maybe you're a bit too boisterous for him?" Misty suggested.

"What do you mean?" asked Takara.

"Well, being a werewolf and a sorceress, you do so much. Does he even know about the other stuff you've been doing?" replied Misty.

"Like how you thought you could be a crime fighter?" Amy asked.

Takara thought back to that one incident in Japan where she had wrestled a goblin mugger in an alleyway in werewolf form who by gunpoint had demanded that an elderly red panda lady with white hair hand over a handbag. The elderly lady stood horrified that Takara then ripped his arms off. Takara then stood and turned to the elderly lady.

"There you go! I saved your handbag! No need to thank me!" Takara smiled her fangs while covered in blood.

The elderly red panda lady then sprayed pepper spray into Takara's eyes.

"AHHHH! AAAHHHHHHHHHHHH !! " Takara fell to the ground in pain. Using her magic she teleported to her flat and put lots of water in a cloth on her eye.

Takara then stopped thinking about this and thought of her answer.

"I think I'll save that one when we know each other a little more better." Takara giggled nervously.

"Does he also know about your prostitution and how many men you've been with?" Misty asked.

"Yes....you have had sex with quite a wide variety of species in your werewolf form. Ogres, minotaurs, griffins, am I missing anything?" Amy pointed out.

Misty thought it over. "One time was a centaur." She suggested.

"Plus you say yourself that all this was just so you'd have some extra money for a rainy day." Amy frowned.

"Does Dougal also know about your wrestling? In events in clubs and bars?" Misty asked.

"Yeah...how's your title as "The Painstorm." going? Asked Amy.

"Pretty good actually, but I haven't told him yet." Replied Takara "Doh…the poor guy's so shy and insecure.

I've asked if he could become a werewolf like me. But he's turned it down. He says he doesn't want to be intimidating and while I haven't suggested that crime incident to him, I have suggested we could become crime fighters."

"What'd he say?" asked Misty.

"Too much work and no time for video games." Takara frowned.

"That's Dougal." Smiled Amy.

"I've thought that maybe I could make him incredibly ill to the point of dying, and that turning him into a werewolf would cure his disease. Maybe that would improve our love life as being a werewolf makes you extra horny. Do you two have any magic like that?"

"Make Dougal sick to the point of dying? Immoral." Amy frowned.

"We don't, but I know just the person." Misty grinned.

Amy shot Misty a very displeased look "MISTY!"

Misty turned to Amy "What? This'll be good for him. He'll be so much more confident, so much less shy. Plus, he'll have a sex drive. Do you want a break up and the ability to never see him again?"

Amy thought it over. "Of course not." She answered.

"Plus, like you I had difficulty keeping dates! Last thing I want is to go back to that life." Said Takara in disgust.

Misty explained her idea. "Back in England we knew a magician by the name of Merloch. He had the power to summon magic potions. He could do potions that could make people grow beards faster, make potions that would make you grow taller, as well as causing diseases by potions he can also cure them. He's amazing!"

"Merloch? I think I know him, lives in Benthrope right?" asked Takara.

"You know him?" Amy asked.

"Yeh….he's given me a nice energy potion, makes you feel like you've just slept 8 hours. I took it just earlier."

"How come?" Misty asked.

"Do you have any idea what the time zones in Japan and Canada are like? Friggin' nightmare!" Takara closed her eyes in frustration.

"Regardless let's go see him!" Misty got up from her seat.

The three teleported off to see Merloch.

END OF CHAPTER 3

Chapter 4

Meanwhile while all this was going on the same day Dougal was attending another day at work.

When he came home, he was surprised to find an anthropomorphic muscular white lion there. He was dressed in a shirt, red tie and wore a black business suit jacket and trousers. He was wearing sunglasses.

Dougal raised an eyebrow. He didn't look like a reporter. He wasn't carrying a mike or a camera.

The lion greeted Dougal. "Hi there. You're Dougal, I believe?

"Er….Hello. Just so you know I did pay my taxes."

"That's not what I'm here for." The white lion frowned.

"Do you want to see my TV license? It's inside…

The lion interrupted Dougal. "That's not what I want either! I'm Shun Sakai. I'm a monster hunter. Here's my business card. I made an English one for you. I'm from Japan." Shun handed Dougal a business card.

"Errr….nice to meet you." Dougal put the card in his work uniform trouser pocket. "How can I help you?"

"I hear you've been dating a werewolf named Takara Tazima. I'd like to talk about her."

"What did she do?" Dougal began to get alarmed. "Did she kill someone?"

"No, not recently anyway and they're always bad people when she does, she's been involved in various illegal activities. Illegal Street fighting competitions, prostitution and drug taking."

Dougal's eyes widened. "GOOD GOD ! ! "

"Yes, she's an unusual case even for me. Most werewolves I pick off are to prevent a curse being spread further and to protect livestock on farms. We have a wild werewolf here, but on different cases. She's a wild girl who abuses her power. The police have hired me to keep an eye on her, I'm a powerful magician just like her."

"Just keep an eye on her? Not arrest her?" said a baffled Dougal.

"She's bribed the law on multiple accounts, the police say they have a field day when she bribes them. Plus being a sorceress, she's a very powerful werewolf to stop, she's injured multiple fighting opponents, every time I stop her, she's gone with me peacefully, only to just bribe the law."

"How nice of her." Dougal frowned.

"If you ever feel your life is in danger, give me a call." Shun looked at Dougal solemnly.

"I will." Dougal replied.

"Have a nice day, Dougal-san." The white lion walked off.

Dougal just stood wondering what to make of everything. To Dougal, Takara seemed to act mostly harmless to him…

END OF CHAPTER 4.

Chapter 5

Amy, Misty and Takara teleported to just outside Merloch's home in Benthrope, England.

Thankfully although it was around 2:14 pm in Canada it was now 7: 14 pm in Britain.

Misty rang the doorbell of Merloch's huge mansion. A white haired and bearded elderly man wearing a blue robe named Merloch answered the door. "Yes?" he said.

"Merloch, baby!" Takara grinned. "Let's do business."

Merloch got annoyed at this. "It's after my working hours."

"Oh…c'mon surely you want that nice second new hot tub you've been after for your swimming pool." Takara smiled. "Your parties haven't been that much of a hit with your one hot tub."

"Ugh…..fine. What do you want?" Merloch growled.

"Two potions, one for curing disease and one for causing a deadly disease." Takara explained simply.

"Whoa, that's extreme stuff you're asking. Are you trying to take over a country?" Merloch asked.

"No....I want to poison my boyfriend, turn him into a werewolf to cure his disease and to give him a higher sex drive, and keep the cure potion as a back up in case that fails." Takara explained simply again.

"Well as this is extreme stuff, I can't sell to just anybody, I'd like a million gold coins for both potions."

"Nuts....I've only got a little over twenty seven thousand." Takara groaned.

"Then stop wasting my time!" Merloch slammed the door.

"Rude!" Misty snarled.

"I'll pay. My husband's a wrestler, he makes tons of money!" Amy said to Takara.

"You'd do that for me?" Takara grinned at Amy.

"Yeh, plus I can just duplicate the money, I have a duplicate spell."

"Why do you need someone hardworking if you can just duplicate money? Takara asked.

It's the fact that he's serious and willing to work hard, that's what counts! Plus he has huge muscles!" Amy replied.

"Merloch! We got the money!" Misty shouted.

Merloch opened the door again. "We're talking business." He smiled. "You said you were poisoning your boyfriend to give him a higher sex drive, right?"

"Right."

"Give the potion to him in a week. It'll look too obvious if you poison him right away." Merloch advised.

"Thanks for the advice." Amy smiled.

"Looks like there's some good in everyone." Misty also smiled.

"Doohhhh…..but I'll be so horny!" Takara groaned.

"Fine, I'll throw in an issue of "Ogre hunks" magazine. Left behind by one of my party guests. Never came back for it."

"Hmmm…..I don't know." Responded Takara.

"It has Azarug Grolluz on the cover." Frowned Merloch.

"Deal!" Amy, Misty and Takara all said at once. The three girls looked at each other.

"It's for me!" Takara got annoyed.

"Fine." Amy sighed. Amy and Takara then look at Misty solemnly.

"Alright….what a bummer." Misty folded her arms.

The girls paid Merloch and left him to the pleasure of his robot prostitute servant.

END OF CHAPTER 5

Chapter 6

A week passed of small chat and taking things easy.

Takara even thought she could give Dougal a chance and not poison him. Takara showed Dougal some of her harmless magic tricks which improved their relationship, however in the week there was non-pleasurable sex.

Takara had sex Dougal once in her human form in her bed in Japan. But the fact that he took Viagra was a huge turn off.

Also, Dougal's cock would be far more pleasurable as a werewolf's and not a human's. So, for the rest of the week, she used her ogre hunks magazine.

A week later Takara decided whether to make her move or not. She was going to poison some delicious noodle soup and give it to Dougal.

"I can't do it." She told Amy and Misty outside the café in Canada where they usually met.

"Why not?" Misty asked.

"It'll look too obvious. He'll realize I'm on to him. I already told you about Shun Sakai, a monster hunter stalking me right?

"Yeh." Amy replied.

"Right." Misty answered.

"I found out from Dougal than Shun Sakai talked to him, and he was told of my crimes. He knows I'm a wild girl now."

"Hmmm…..can I make a suggestion?" Misty asked.

"You may."

"Why don't you just tip the poison in his cola when he's out at work? Cook the soup WITHOUT the poison and if he tips it out or something you can guilt him into sex?" Misty grinned.

"Hmmm…think I'll only use part of that plan. I'm not wasting good soup! Nice suggestion, though."

"Hey, no problem."

END OF CHAPTER 6

Chapter 7

Takara followed out Misty's plan. One day while he was at work, she teleported into Dougal's flat and poisoned a bottle of his cola, a nearly empty bottle that would be disposed of quickly for safety.

A few days later, in Takara's flat in Japan, Takara was reading the Japanese version of the magazine "Ogre Hunks." (Yes, they had businesses in Britain, the USA and Japan.) She was in human form. When suddenly her phone rang. Seeing it was Dougal, she replied in an English voice.

"Hey, sweetie." She smiled.

"Takara…(COUGH)…..I don't think (COUGH) I can see you tonight…(COUGH)…..I really….really….don't feel well."

Takara tried to put on a sad voice while grinning "Awww…..I'm so sorry to hear that. What's wrong?"

"I've got purple spots all over me, a really high temperature, green spots on my tongue, I'm dizzy plus I'm coughing a lot. I tried to call NHS 111. That's a medical phone line you call in Britain if you think you're very ill. I tried to find out what was wrong with me. But they're too busy."

"Chances are they'd just say. "Kiss your butt goodbye." Takara thought still grinning.

"I'm really scared. What have I got!? Am I gonna die!?" Dougal panicked.

"Not with me around you won't! I'm coming around!"

"Takara, no! You'll catch the disease!"

"I will not. I'm a werewolf remember?"

"Oh right."

Takara put the cure potion in a brown backpack which she then wore. She thought about wearing a sexy nurse's outfit, but she figured that would make Dougal realize she poisoned him.

"Rats." Takara frowned. "I gotta put the hormone patrol to the side. Put it on leave for a bit." Takara teleported to Dougal's flat.

She saw Dougal in his pyjamas in his bed. Dougal looked everything that he had said over the phone plus more. He was white as a sheet.

"Whoa." Takara gritted her teeth. "You look like shit."

"Thanks for (COUGH) pointing out the bloody obvious! What's wrong with me!?"

"Hmmm…..I don't know. Let's take your temperature." Takara put a thermometer in Dougal's mouth. The round part at the end exploded.

"Whoa. Never seen that before."

"I'M GONNA DIE! I'M DEAD! I'M DEAD! I'M FUCKING DEEEEAAAADDDDDDD ! ! ! " Dougal immediately went into tears.

"Don't panic! We still don't know your disease! It could still be harmless!" Takara tried to calm Dougal.

"WELL, WHAT IS IT!?" Dougal yelled.

"Keep calm. Even if you were dying, I can still cure you, I'll look it up. May I have your internet access?"

"Of course, anything! I have a laptop you can look my disease on."

"Great! Don't get up, stay in bed." Takara went to Dougal's laptop in his kitchen and living room and turned it on.

"As if (COUGH) I have a choice with this dizziness!" Dougal snarled.

"What's your passcode?" Takara called to Dougal.

"(COUGH) 0250." Dougal said simply.

After Takara did some typing around on Dougal's laptop. She went up reading about Dougal's disease on multiple websites. She read up about the deaths it caused.

"DAMN!" she thought her eyes widened deciding not to say the word out loud.

"Alright, I found what you got." Takara called to Dougal and walked to his bedroom.

"WELL!?" Dougal cried completely terrified.

"You have the purple spot plague. One of the last instances of the disease was on an island populated of gargoyles a short to medium distance from Somalia, 42 years ago. It caused 34 deaths.

Dougal just stared blankly without saying a word. The word "plague" and "deaths" did not spell good news.

Takara saw Dougal's reaction and tried to comfort him. "Dougal? Dougal?" Takara waved her hand in front of Dougal's eyes. "Get a grip! I can cure you!"

"H-how?" Dougal hugged himself shaking.

"I can turn you into a werewolf. The stronger immune system will fight your disease."

"There…..has to be (COUGH) another way. Can't you get somebody who can cure me?"

"Yeh, but have you seen their prices? Utter rip off. Literally millions of gold coins."

"I'm up diarrhoea creek without a paddle."

"No, you're not. Let me turn you into a werewolf."

"There must be another way."

"You have as much options as farting loudly in a school classroom or in a quiet church with some people and an echo."

"I guess....I have no other option." Dougal sighed.

"You got any cough medicine? It'll help a little bit once you're a wolf. Also do you mind if I get a glass of water to get over this shock."

"Yeh, glasses and medicine are in the cupboard next to the cooker."

Takara went to Dougal's living room and took her magic spectre and book from her backpack. She then took her cure potion and turned on the tap of the kitchen sink to drown out the small noise of her pouring some of the potion into some cough medicine. After taking a drink of water and turning off the tap. She put the cough medicine in her backpack and went over to Dougal with her magic book and sceptre.

She was going to say the words needed to turn Dougal into a werewolf.

"Magic!" She shouted. "Teleport Dougal to inside my bed in Japan!"

Dougal teleported to Takara's bed. Takara herself then teleported to Japan. She didn't get in bed with Dougal though.

"Why did (COUGH) you teleport me to your bed?" Dougal asked taking off his glasses figuring they would be damaged by his new form. He set his glasses to the side.

"Way more space. You'll be much bigger as a werewolf. Magic, turn Dougal into a werewolf!"

POOF!

Immediately Dougal turned into a huge grey muscular wolf. His clothes disappeared but his brown hair still remained. His clothes didn't rip off. They just disappeared. He still looked unwell. The purple spots still showed through his fur.

"Let me give you some cough medicine. It may help."

"Sure." Dougal groaned weakly.

Takara gave Dougal some medicine.

"Do you feel any better?" Takara asked.

"No."

"Well….in the mean time." Takara smiled. "Let me keep you warm. You need warmth!"

Takara transformed into her werewolf form and climbed in bed with Dougal, hoping that in time his disease would clear up.

"How can you think of sex at a time like this!?" Dougal snarled.

"It's not sex. I'm just keeping you warm."

"Oh…okay."

Within a few hours to Takara's relief, Dougal's disease cleared up. He was now a werewolf and Takara's sex slave.

END OF CHAPTER 7

Chapter 8

Time passed. After a little over a week had passed, and after some arrangements, Dougal was finally going to meet up with his old friends.

Outside a posh coffee shop and café in Canada, Amy and Misty stood waiting for Takara and Dougal.

"She's finally got Dougal to come along to see us. Never thought I'd see the day." Misty smiled.

"Yes, Dougal's still a little shook up from the disease that nearly took his life, though." Amy replied.

"I'm not surprised." Misty replied. "That and the fact he's a werewolf now."

"Yep, so no pranks on Dougal." Amy said sternly to Misty.

Misty rolled her eyes. "Fine, I'll take the tacks off his chair." Misty brushed Dougal's chair and took the tacks.

Takara showed up with Dougal both in their human forms. Dougal was a bit pale, had bags under his eyes like he hadn't been sleeping and held his arms around himself hugging himself.

"Long time, no see wolf boy." Amy smiled. She got up and hugged Dougal. "So glad to have you as my friend again."

"We had such great times with you." Misty smiled. "I still have that manga you lent me as a teenager of the talking robot cat with the jetpack and armed shoulder rockets. You never asked for that back."

Takara showed Dougal to a seat. "Sit down and I'll get us our drinks. Amy, Misty what will you have?"

"Cappuccino." Amy replied.

"Iced Latte." Misty replied.

Takara turned to Dougal. "And you, Dougal, what will you have?"

"How about the hot chocolate with marshmallows, as you mentioned they have?" Dougal answered.

"Nice choice. I'll be right back." Takara walked off leaving Dougal with Amy and Misty.

"He finally shows his face. How's life been for the new wolf boy?" Misty teased.

"Stressful, and don't call me wolf boy." Dougal said in an annoyed voice. He gave Misty a dirty look.

"What's stressful about having super strength, a nice fur coat for the winter, being able to breathe ice beams and lightning and intimidating your enemies?" Misty asked.

"How about when you intimidate your enemies. They will look for new and more extreme ways to fight back even if they fail a lot? Ask anyone who's fought in a war." Dougal frowned.

"Regardless you're still mostly in the right. Takara says she hopes to finally settle down and stop doing so much…wild stuff. Haven't you noticed her settling down and being so much laid back now?" Amy asked.

"Wonderful. Doesn't stop a monster hunter from stalking both of us." Dougal sulked.

"I think he's only stalking Takara. Takara said you broke into tears and yelled "I'm so horrible!" when Shun said he feared you would abuse your new power." Misty giggled.

"That's supposed to make me feel better?" Dougal sulked.

"You can fight back to a decent level to your enemies, don't eat me, wolf boy." Misty smiled.

"Don't you have that reflect spell that would backfire on me if I did?" Dougal asked.

"Oh, we don't use that spell anymore." Misty replied. "Amy and I thought it made life too easy and boring. We've been using Vulgarth's gym to toughen ourselves up and give our enemies a fighting chance!"

Dougal thought it over. "Hmm....I did think you both looked slightly different."

Misty turned to Amy. "I've got stronger arms than you, Amy!"

"No competition there, you've always had longer arms that go nearly all the way to your feet."

"Yeh, I just realized I have really long arms." Misty frowned.

"You're half human that's why. Mum was a human. Elves are usually a short to medium height. But being half human made me tall and you short with long arms." Amy replied.

"WHAT!?" Misty shouted. "I'M A FREAK!"

"Now who's got self-esteem issues." Dougal smiled.

"Shut it!" Misty growled at Dougal and then turned to Amy. "That's why you're taller than Dad?" Misty asked Amy.

"Yep."

"AAHHHHH!"

"Get over it! Life could be worse!" Dougal replied to Misty.

"Ugh....I suppose." Misty folded her arms. "I suppose life will get better for you."

"I guess, I thought being a werewolf would get me fired from my job. But Takara talked to Ramsey my boss."

"What happened?" Amy asked.

"She said to accept my new condition or else he would have to suffer a type of magnet curse in which rocks would lift off the ground and hit him in the groin."

Amy gritted her teeth. Misty shuddered.

"Painful." Amy spoke through her teeth.

"I don't understand it, my immune system's always been pretty good. I rarely catch a cold. How is it I suddenly catch a deadly disease with little to no warning?" Dougal sighed.

"Life works in strange ways." Misty replied and gave a nervous smile.

Amy tried to comfort Dougal. "Yeh…..in 1422 a deadly plague nearly wiped out an island full of trolls. I think it was an island a short distance from Mexico…or was it Suriname? I think another deadly disease was on another island a short to medium distance from that country too. 1382 it took place I think."

"But cheer up! You survived! And we're all friends again!" Misty cheered.

"Listen, we were wondering if you could help us write a fourth entry to Mega Elven Twins or whatever the too damn long title is." Amy said to Dougal.

"Yeh…..do you think Mavis should settle down with Firethorn the Demon Lord? He's a nice guy and despite his name he's not really from hell."

"Two things. One. I've been thinking about writing more serious things and two, I haven't read the other books." Dougal replied.

"You haven't? But Brenda's a great character. I love it when she calls Clawdia a fish faced cunt who should be maimed by large plastic spoons and shat on by a fat piece of shit who ate at Taco Bell! She's named after my middle name." Misty laughed.

"Again, I had no involvement in the sequels!" Dougal replied.

"You should read them; I can get you some copies." Amy smiled.

"I also told you; I want to write more serious things." Dougal frowned.

"Such as?" Amy asked.

"A murder mystery or…..something." Dougal struggled.

"Right. Have you ever watched anything other than cartoons, comedies and sitcoms?" Amy teased.

"I can learn! And yes, I have!" Dougal snapped.

"Alright, you write what you feel." Amy patted his hand. "Don't let us stop you."

Takara returned with the drinks. "Here we all go. You three getting along?"

"Just fine." Dougal replied.

"How's life been for the new werewolf couple?" Misty asked.

"Wonderful! Dougal's so beautiful as a werewolf, beautiful grey coat, huge tail plus I never thought he'd be taller than me from some of the werewolves I've seen! He's amazingly huge! His eyesight has improved as a werewolf! No need for glasses!"

"I'll have difficulty moving around my home every time there's a full moon!" Dougal sulked.

"Come to my flat. There's plenty of room! In my bed!" Takara grinned to Dougal.

"Takara thinks you're beautiful now!" Amy smiled. "Isn't that great?"

"Plus, he pleases me so much in bed now! He gives the best cuddles after sex!"

"Way to go, you beautiful beast!" Misty grinned.

"But don't you love me for my human side?" Dougal asked.

"Course I do! I wouldn't have stuck around if I didn't!" Takara patted Dougal's hand.

"You have a sex drive now! Aren't you proud?" Misty beamed.

"I…guess…" Dougal said quietly and thought it over.

"His sex drive has only increased slightly though. According to my spell book it seems there's something I misread. It only increases your sex drive slightly." Takara explained.

Dougal raised an eyebrow. "Wait so even before your werewolf curse, you were regularly horny!?"

"Yeh.....ain't that weird? Regardless you now act like a normal dude. Almost. You're still low but not REALLY low in the sex drive department."

"I'm a werewolf now and you call this normal!?"

"In a land full of talking animals and several creatures such as ogres, elves, goblins and trolls. Yes, it is!"

"There's no point moping about it. What's done is done." Amy pointed out.

"You could remove my curse. You have spells for removing magic spells and curses cast on people."

"No way! Takara loves the new you!" Amy refused.

"I won't be a great werewolf! I'm still wimpy! I've refused to be a crime fighter! In a bank robbery I'd probably just call the police if given the chance!"

"A werewolf calling the police for a bank robbery. Why do I find that humorous?" asked Misty still smiling.

"True, but as you say yourself, you're not immortal and you could get hurt. And then you told me the news story of the werewolf in India who tried to be heroic but was shot dead by terrorists. You're so thoughtful. And you made me see how irresponsible I was. I still remember the cuts I got street fighting. Did I ever tell you one time I took on three goblins armed with knives. Lucky to survive.

Dougal's eyes widened. "Good god! I don't care what the spell book says about how you retain most of your personality, by turning yourself into a werewolf, you've changed a lot!"

"I don't regularly eat people. What are you on about?"

"You fight in both legal and non-legal fights, you've had sex for money, you've taken drugs, tried to fight crime despite taking drugs and been arrested multiple times only to bribe the police! You would not have done all this staying human! You've abused power! The only hardcore thing I've done since becoming a werewolf is fight urges not to drink from a toilet!"

"Then help me settle, Dougal. Keep me satisfied. Stay a wolf and keep me on the right track."

"Do it." Amy cheered.

"Do it!" Misty also cheered.

Dougal sighed. "Fine." He said.

"That's my boy. Now let me have a kiss."

"Alright."

Takara gave Dougal a peck on the cheek.

Dougal closed his eyes. "What have I got myself into?"

HE END OF BOOK 4.

That was the last one!

Thank you for reading. Many times I have thought about doing a sequel to this and also with a prequel series called "The five oddballs." which focus on the characters being unpopular kids in school and Amy having to use her magic as kids. But that's all writer's block. I don't know if I'll ever conquer it, but thank you for reading.
If you enjoyed this series of stories. I have a fanfiction account where I wrote 125 fanfiction stories. The few positive reviews I received were the inspiration for me to write this. Even my bad flawed stories had positive reviews. My fanfiction account is Super Fanfic Entertainment.
Amy the elf sorceress and her friends also started out as a webcomic on my Deviantart account called "Ilovecomicstrips45." The comic is just called Amy the elf. The comics are non-canon to the stories in this and the characters are developed differently.

Milton Keynes UK
Ingram Content Group UK Ltd.
UKHW022128291124
451915UK00010B/577